FALLING FOR THE MARSHAL

DONNA ALWARD

When Jen had informed her of this particular booking, Maggie had lost her cool instead of thanking her daughter for actually taking some initiative with the business. Instead she'd harped about her ruined vacation plans.

She should just let the resentment go. Mexico wasn't going anywhere. She'd go another time, that was all. And the money from this off-season booking would come in handy come summer, when repairs to the house would need to be undertaken.

The marshal was a guest here and it was her job to make him feel welcome. Even if she had her doubts. A cop, of all people. He was probably rigid and scheduled and had no sense of humour.

Letting out a breath and pasting on her "greeting" smile, she went to the door and opened it before he had a chance to ring the bell.

"Welcome to Mountain Haven B&B," she got out, but the rest of her rehearsed greeting flew out of her head as she stared a long way up into blue-green eyes.

"Thank you." His lips moved above a grey and black parka that was zipped precisely to the top. "I know it's off season, and I appreciate your willingness to open for me. I hope it hasn't inconvenienced you."

It was a struggle to keep her mouth from dropping open, to keep the welcome smile curving her lips. His introductory speech had locked her gaze on his face, and she was staggered. She'd be spending the next three weeks with *this* man? In an otherwise empty bed and breakfast? Jennifer would only be here another few days, and then it was back to school. It would be just the two of them.

What had started out as an annoying business necessity was now curled with intimacy. He was, very possibly, the most gorgeous man she'd ever seen. Even bundled in winter gear she sensed his lean, strong build. His voice was smooth with just a hint of gravel, giving it a rumbling texture; the well-shaped lips were unsmiling despite his polite speech. And he had killer eyes...eyes that gleamed brilliantly in contrast to his dark clothing.

"I am in the right place, aren't I?" He turned his head and looked at the truck, then back at her, his brows pulling together a bit as she remained stupidly silent.

Pull yourself together, she told herself. She stepped back, opening the door wider to welcome him in. "If you're Nathaniel Griffith, you're in the right place."

He smiled finally, a quick upturn of the lips, and exhaled, a cloud forming in the frigid air. "That's a relief. I was afraid I'd gotten lost. And please..." He pulled off his glove and held out his hand. "Call me Nate. I only get called Nathaniel when I'm in trouble with my boss or my mother."

She smiled back, genuinely this time, as she shook his hand. It was warm and firm and enveloped her smaller fingers completely. She couldn't imagine him in trouble for anything. He looked like Mr. All-American.

"I'm Maggie Taylor, the owner. Please, come in. I'll show you your room and get you familiar with the place."

"I'll just get my bags," he said, stepping back outside the door.

unless of course you have a cell." Maggie dismissed the futility of trying to draw him out and gave him the basic run-down instead. "There's no television in your room, but there is a den downstairs that you're welcome to use."

Maggie paused. Nate was waiting patiently for her to finish her spiel. It was very odd, with him being her only guest. Knowing he'd be the only guest for the next few weeks. It didn't seem right, telling him mealtimes and rules.

She softened her expression. "Look, normally there's a whole schedule thing with meals and everything, but you're my only guest. I think we can be a little more flexible. I usually serve breakfast between eight and nine, so if that suits you, great. I can work around your plans. Dinner is served at six-thirty. For lunch, things are fluid. I can provide it or not, for a minimum charge on your overall bill. I'm happy to provide you with local areas of interest, and you have wifi in your room."

Nate tucked his hands into his jeans pockets. "I'm your only guest?"

"That's right. It's not my busiest time right now."

"Then…" his eyes met hers sheepishly. "Look, I'm going to feel awkward eating alone. I don't suppose…we could all eat together."

Nate watched her closely and she felt colour creep into her cheeks yet again. Silly Jennifer and her sugges-tive comments. The front side *was* as attractive as the back and Maggie couldn't help but notice as they stood together in the quiet room. It wasn't how things were usually done. Normally guests ate in the dining room and she ate at the nook or she and Jen at the kitchen table. Yet it would seem odd, serving him all alone in the dining room. It was antisocial, somehow. Despite the ideas Jen put in her head, Maggie knew it was her job to make his stay comfortable.

She struggled to keep her voice low and even. "Basically, your stay should be enjoyable. If you prefer to eat with us, that would be fine. And if there's anything I can do to make your stay more comfortable, let me know."

"Everything here looks great, Ms. Taylor."

"Then I'll leave you to unpack. The bathroom is two doors down, and as my only guest it's yours alone. Jennifer and I each have our own so you won't have to share. I'll be downstairs. Let me know if there's anything you need. Otherwise, I'll see you for dinner."

She courteously shut the door, then leaned against it, closing her eyes. Nate Griffith wasn't an ordinary guest, that much she knew already. She couldn't shake the irrational feeling that he was hiding something. He hadn't said or done anything to really make her think so, beyond being proprietary with his backpack. But something niggled at the back of her mind, something that made her uncomfortable. Given his profession, she should be reassured. Who could be safer than someone in law enforcement? Why would he have any sort of ulterior motive?

His good looks were something she'd simply have to ignore. She'd have to get over her silly awkwardness in a hurry, since they were going to be essentially roommates for the next few weeks. Jen wouldn't be here to run interference much longer, and Maggie would rely on her normal professional, warm persona. Piece of cake.

He was just a man, after all. A man on vacation from a stressful job. A man with an expense account that would make up for her lost plans by helping pay for her next trip.

———

NATE HEAVED OUT A SIGH AS THE DOOR SHUT WITH A firm click. Thank goodness she was gone.

He looked around the room. Very nice. Grant had ensured him that the rural location didn't mean substandard lodging, and so far he was right. What he'd seen of the house was clean, warm, and welcoming. His room was no different.

The furniture was sturdy golden pine; the spread on the bed was thick and looked homemade with its country design in navy, burgundy, deep green and cream. An extra blanket in rich red lay over the foot of the bed. He ran his hand over the footboard. He would have preferred no footboard, so he could stretch out. But it didn't matter. What mattered was that he was here and he had all the amenities he needed. To anyone in the area, he'd be a vacationing guest. To his superiors, he'd be consistently connected through the internet and in liaison with local authorities. Creature comforts were secondary, but not unwelcome. Lord knew he'd stayed in a lot worse places while on assignment.

He unpacked his duffle, laying clothing neatly in the empty dresser drawers. His hand paused on a black sweater. When Grant had mentioned a bed and break-fast, Nate had instantly thought of some middle-aged couple. When he'd learned Maggie ran Mountain Haven alone, he'd pictured a woman in her mid-to-late forties who crocheted afghans for the furniture and exchanged recipes for chicken pot pie with her guests. Maggie Taylor didn't fit his profile at all. Neither did Jen. He'd known she was here, but she seemed preco-cious and typically teenage. Certainly not the kind to get in trouble with the police.

He rested his hips on the curved footboard and frowned. It was hard to discern Maggie's age. Initially he'd thought her maybe a year or two older than himself. But the appearance of her nearly grown daughter had changed that impression. He couldn't tell for sure, but she had to be at least late thirties to have a daughter that age. Yet...her skin was still creamy and unlined, her eyes blue with thick lashes. Her hand had been much smaller than his, and soft.

But it was Maggie's eyes that stuck in his mind. Eyes that smiled warmly with welcome but that held a hint of cool caution in their depths. Eyes that told him what-ever her path had been, it probably hadn't been an easy one.

He stood up abruptly and reached for the jeans in his duffle, going to hang them in the closet. He wasn't here to make calf-eyes at the proprietress. That was the last thing he should be thinking about. He had a job to do. That was all. He had information to gather and who better to ask than someone in the know, someone who would take his questions for tourist curiosity? Inviting himself to dinner had put her on the spot, but with the desired results.

The afternoon light was already starting to wane when he dug out his laptop and set it up on the small desk to the left of the bed. Within seconds it was booted up, connected and ready to go. He logged in with his password, checked his e-mail…and waited for everything to download. Once he'd taken care of everything that needed his immediate attention, he quickly composed a few short notes, hitting the send button. Now he just had to wait for the requested reply. He tapped his fingers on the desk. Waiting was not something he did well.

But perhaps learning to wait was a life lesson he needed. He'd been one to act first and think later too many times. Dealing with the aftermath of mistakes had caused him to be put on leave in the first place. He hadn't even been two weeks into his leave when it had been cut short and he'd been given this assignment, and he was glad of it. He wasn't one to sit around twiddling his thumbs.

Grant had asked for him personally. As a favour. And this wasn't a job to be rushed. It was a time for watching and waiting.

He frowned at the monitor and his empty inbox. For now, his laptop was his connection to the outside world. It was a tiny community. The less conspicuous he was, the better.

He realized that his room had grown quite dark and checked his watch. It was after six already, and Maggie had said dinner was at six-thirty. He didn't want to get things off to a bad start on his first day, so he shut down the laptop and put his backpack beneath the empty duffel in the closet.

———

MAGGIE HEARD HIS FOOTSTEPS MOVING ABOUT UPSTAIRS for a long time, and listened to the muffled thump as she mixed dough and browned ground beef for the soup.

Nate Griffith. U.S. Marshal. The name had conjured an image of a flat-faced cop when Jennifer had told her about the reservation. Despite the flashes of coolness, he was anything but. He couldn't be more than thirty, thirty-one. And it hadn't taken but a moment to realize he was all legs and broad shoulders, and polite manners.

"Whatcha making?"

Jennifer's voice interrupted and for once Maggie was glad of it. She'd already spent too long thinking about her latest lodger.

"Pasta e fagioli and foccacia bread."

"Excellent." Jen grabbed a cookie from a beige pottery jar and leaned against the counter, munching.

Maggie watched her. There were some days she really missed the pre-teen years. Parenting had been so much simpler then. Yet hard as it was, she hated to see Jen leave again.

"Day after tomorrow, huh. Did you book your bus ticket?"

"I booked it return when I came, remember?" She reached in the jar for another cookie.

"You'll spoil your supper," Maggie warned.

Jen simply raised an eyebrow as if to say, *I'm not twelve, Mother.*

"You should be glad I'm leaving. That leaves you alone with Detective Hottie."

Maggie glared.

"Oh, come on, Mom. He's a little old for me, even if he is a fine specimen. But he's just about right for you."

Maggie put the spoon down with more force than she intended. "First of all, keep your voice down. He is a paying guest in this house." She ignored the flutter that skittered through her at Jen's attempt at matchmaking. "He wouldn't be here at all if you'd asked first and booked later."

Jennifer stopped munching. "You're still mad about that, huh."

Maggie sighed, forgetting all about his footsteps. It wasn't all Jen's fault. She did her own share of picking fights. She should be trying to keep Jen close, not pushing her away.

"I just wish…I wish you'd give some thought to things first, instead of racing headlong and then having to backtrack. You took the reservation without even consulting me."

"I was trying to help. I told you I was sorry about it. And they did come through with the cash, so what's the big deal?"

How could Maggie explain that the big deal was that she worried over Jen day and night? She hadn't been blind the last few years. Jen had skated through without getting seriously hurt. Yet. But she'd had her share of trouble and Maggie was terrified that one day she'd get a phone call that something truly serious had happened. She wished Jen took it as seriously as she did.

"Let's not argue about it anymore, okay?" Arguing over the reservation was irrelevant now. Maggie had been irritated with Jennifer at the time for not taking a credit card number, but it had ceased to matter. The United States Marshals Service was picking up the tab. All of it. A day after Nate had reserved the room, someone from his office had called and made arrangements for payment, not even blinking when she'd told them the rate, or the cost of extras. And she'd charged them high season rates, just because she'd been so put out at having to put her travel plans on hold.

She pressed dough into two round pans, dimpling the tops with her fingers before putting them under a tea towel to rise. No matter how much she wished she were lying on a beach in Cancun right now, she still derived pleasure from doing what she did best. Cooking for one was a dull, lonely procedure and her spirits lightened as she added ingredients to the large stockpot on the stove. Jen had been home for the last week, but it wasn't the same now that she was nearly adult and spreading her wings. Having guests meant having someone else to do for. It was why she'd chosen a B&B in the first place.

The footsteps halted above her, the house falling completely silent as their argument faltered.

"I didn't mean to pick a fight with you."

"Me either." Jen shuffled to the kitchen doorway and Maggie longed to mend fences, although she didn't know how.

"Supper in an hour," she called gently, but it went ignored.

Maggie reached across the counter to turn on the radio. She hummed quietly with a recent country hit as she turned her attention to pastry. Her foot tapped along with the beat until she slid everything into the oven, added tiny tubes of pasta to the pot, and cleaned up the cooking mess, the process of cooking and cleaning therapeutic.

At precisely six-twenty, he appeared at the kitchen door.

She turned with the bread pans in her hands, surprised to see him there. Again, she felt a warning thump at his presence. Why in the world was she reacting this way to a complete stranger? It was more than a simple admiration of his good looks. A sliver of danger snuck down her spine. She knew nothing about him. He looked like a normal, nice guy. But how would she know? She didn't even know the reason why he was on a leave of absence. What could have happened to make him need to take extended time off? Suddenly all her misgivings, ones she rarely gave credence to, came bubbling up to the surface. Most of the time she was confident in her abilities to look after herself. Something about Nate Griffith challenged that. And very soon, it would just be the two of them in the house.

"Is something wrong?"

She shook her head, giving a start and putting the pans down on top of the stove. "No, not at all. You just surprised me." Maggie took a deep breath, keeping her back to him. "Dinner's not quite ready. It won't be long."

"Is there anything I can do to help?"

He took a few steps into the kitchen. It was her job to make him at ease and feel at home, so why on earth was she finding it so difficult? She forced a smile as she flipped the round loaves out of the pans and on to a cooling rack. "Jen should be down soon. Besides, it's my job to look after you, remember?"

"Well, sure." He leaned easily against the side of the refrigerator. "But I thought we were going to play it a little less formal."

He had her there. She thought for a moment as she got the dishes out of the cupboard. He was only here for a few weeks. What harm could come of being friendly, after all? Her voices of doubt were just being silly; she was making something out of nothing. He'd be gone back to his job and the palm trees before she knew it.

"All right." She held out bread plates and bowls. "Informal it is. We can use the kitchen or the dining room, whichever you prefer. If you could set the table with these, I'll finish up here."

He pushed himself upright with an elbow. "Absolutely." He moved to take the dishes and their fingers brushed. Without thinking, her gaze darted up to his with alarm. For a second she held her breath. But then he turned away to the table as if nothing had connected.

Only she knew it had. And that was bad, bad news.

2

He'd set the three places at one end of the table: one at the head and the other two flanking it. There was little chance of her getting away with sitting across from him. He'd be close. Too close. With his long legs, their knees might bump under the table. Maggie's pulse fluttered at the thought and she frowned. It wasn't like her to be so twitchy.

As she watched, he lit the thick candles at the centre of the table with the butane lighter.

Maggie paused at the intimacy of the setting and shook it off again, putting the soup tureen on the table. It shouldn't make her feel so threatened, but it did. Even with Jennifer here, a simple dinner had somehow transformed into something more. Maggie simply didn't do relationships of any kind. Not even casual ones. It always ended badly with her being left to try to pick up the pieces. After the last time, with Tom, there hadn't been many pieces left to pick up. She had to hold on to every single one. All that she had left was put into raising

Jennifer and running her business. She didn't know why Nate would go to the bother of setting the atmosphere, and it unsettled her.

"Ms. Taylor?"

Maggie realized she'd been staring at the table. She laughed lightly. "I'm sorry. You were saying?"

"I asked if you ran the Haven alone. I'm afraid I didn't get many details when I booked."

"I do, yes." She brought the basket of bread to the table and invited him to sit with a hand. She was surprised when he waited until she was seated before seating himself. "Jennifer attends school in Edmonton, so she's not around much anymore."

"Which makes you sad."

Maggie smiled, pleasantly surprised by his small, but accurate insight. The house did seem unbearably lonely when Jen was gone. "Despite teenage angst and troubles, yes, it does. I miss having her close by. Speaking of, she should be here by now."

She pushed her chair back and stood, fluttering a hand when he made a similar move out of courtesy. "It's okay. Jen knows to be on time. I'll call her."

Maggie made her way to the bottom of the stairs. What she'd said was true. She did miss having Jen closer, even though at times she was glad Jen was away from here and making new friends. Not all her acquaintances at home were ones Maggie would have chosen. And the last thing Maggie needed was for the marshal to know about Jen's brush with the law.

"Jennifer. Dinner," she called up the stairs.

There was a muffled thump from Jen's room, then

she came down, earbuds still stuck in her ears and her phone stuffed in her pocket.

They went to the kitchen together, but when Jen sat and reached for the bread, Maggie shook her head.

"Not at the table, please."

Jen seemed unconcerned as she plucked the buds from her ears. "Hey, Nate," she greeted, snagging the piece of bread as though it were the most natural thing in the world.

Maggie saw Nate try to hide a smile. Honestly, she wondered sometimes if the manners she'd tried to instill had gone in one ear and out the other.

"Hey, Jennifer." Nate politely answered the greeting and broke the awkwardness by starting a conversation. "So...spring break is just about over. You looking forward to getting back to school?"

Maggie relaxed and ladled soup into bowls. Nate apparently had paid good attention to *his* upbringing. Manners and a natural sense of small talk. And for once, Jen didn't seem to mind answering.

"I guess. It's been kind of boring around here. Nothing to do."

"Oh, I don't know. With all this snow...there must be winter sports. Skiing, skating, tobogganing...or are those things uncool these days?"

Maggie grinned behind her water glass. She'd suggested a day of cross-country skiing earlier in the week, only to have the idea vetoed by Jen. The same Jen who a few years ago would have jumped at the chance.

"I dunno," Jen replied.

Nate nodded. "I'm looking forward to spending lots

of time outdoors," he said. "No snow where I live. This is a real treat for me."

Maggie pictured him bundled up, his boots strapped into a pair of snowshoes, with his eyes gleaming like sapphire bullets beneath his toque. Her heart thumped heavily. His lean, strong build made the outdoors a natural choice.

"I suppose you're all athletic and stuff." Jennifer paused and tilted her head as if examining him.

"It's part of my job. I have to stay in good shape. Just because I'm not...working, doesn't mean I can ignore the routine." He paused to take a spoonful of soup. "Besides, if I eat your mother's cooking for the next two weeks, I'm really going to have to watch my figure." His smile sparkled at Maggie. "This is delicious."

"Thanks," Maggie responded. She was used to receiving polite compliments on her cooking. It made no sense that his praise caused her heart to pitter patter like a schoolgirl's.

She considered steering the conversation so that Jen didn't monopolize it, but she realized two things. Jen was more animated than she'd been the whole break, and Maggie was learning a whole lot more about Nate by sitting back and listening to their exchange.

"So, Nate...when you're not vacationing, what's your job like? Are you like a regular cop or what?" Jen popped a spoonful of soup into her mouth while waiting for his answer.

Nate concentrated on adding grated parmesan to the top of his soup. "No, not like a regular cop. I get to do special stuff. A lot of what I do is finding fugitives, people who have committed crimes and are on the run."

"You mean like "America's Most Wanted"?" Jen leaned forward now, her dinner forgotten.

Nate nodded. "Exactly like that. And sometimes I'm sent out on high profile security details, too."

"Isn't that dangerous?" Maggie's voice intruded. A cop was bad enough, but even she knew that a police officer dealt with a lot of the mundane. This seemed like a whole other level. "Don't you worry about getting killed?"

His eyes were steady on hers. "Yes, but not as much as I worry about getting the job done."

Maggie's chin flattened. Tall, strong, and handsome was one thing, but having a target painted on his chest was quite another. She couldn't imagine anyone choosing such a lifestyle.

"Have you ever killed anyone?"

"Jennifer!" Maggie put down her spoon and glared at her daughter for her crassness in asking such a thing. Nate's eyes made the transition to look at Jennifer, the smile disappearing completely.

"Jen, that was beyond inappropriate." Maggie spoke sharply. "Please apologize."

But Nate shook his head. "There's no need. It's a valid question. I get it a lot." He took a drink of water. "I work as a part of a team. And our goal is to bring fugitives to justice, or to protect those we are assigned to protect. Of course we prefer to bring them in unharmed. But if we're fired upon, we have to fire back."

Silence fell over the table.

Maggie tried to fill the uncomfortable gap the way a hostess should, yet all she could see was Nate, holding a smoking gun. The thought chilled her considerably.

"That must be very stressful."

Nate nodded. "It can be, yes."

Jen's voice interrupted again. "Is that why you're here?"

Maggie kicked her beneath the table. Jen bit down on her lip but watched him, undeterred.

Nate swallowed. "Part of it, yes. I was directed to take some time off after a...particularly challenging case. A little rest and relaxation is just what the doctor ordered."

He smiled, but it wasn't as warm as before. "In keeping with that, I'd appreciate if you'd keep my presence here low-key. I realize it's a small community, but right now I want to enjoy the outdoors and not worry about speculation."

Maggie aimed a stern look at Jennifer before turning to Nate and answering.

"Of course. You are a guest here, and of course we'll respect your wishes. That's what the Haven is all about." At least she didn't have to worry right now. He was on vacation. What he did for a living had no bearing on anything.

"Thank you," he murmured. He picked up his spoon again and resumed eating, and Jennifer wisely let the subject drop for the rest of the meal.

. . .

"DESSERT, MR. GRIFFITH?"

Nate looked up at Maggie as she removed his plate and bowl. The meal had had its uncomfortable moments, but he was actually glad the questions had been asked and answered. He got the feeling that Maggie would have been too polite to ask point-blank what her daughter had. Not only that, but the questions had provided a natural way to introduce his cover. Even if he did feel a bit guilty about the half-lie. He'd deliberately prodded her about some things, like asking if she ran the B&B alone when he knew darn well she did. Still…it was all necessary.

Maggie was waiting, her lips curved pleasantly in what he now realized was her hostess smile. "I shouldn't…but maybe you could tell me what it is first."

Her lips twitched…a good sign, he thought. She'd looked far too serious throughout the rest of the meal. If he could get her to relax a bit, it would go a lot easier towards getting what he needed to know without her feeling like she was being questioned.

"Peach and blueberry tart with ice cream," she answered.

Jennifer clattered about the kitchen, already scooping out servings. "Can't really resist that, now can I," he acquiesced. "So…yes, please. And stop calling me Mr. Griffith. Mr. Griffith is my father or my uncle."

Maggie put on coffee while Jennifer finished doling out servings of the tart, taking hers and escaping to the den and the television. When Maggie placed the dessert before him, the smell alone was enough to remind him of home. Sweets weren't something he indulged in much anymore, but his mother was a fantastic baker and plied him with goodies whenever he visited. Right now the scent of fruit and cinnamon took him back to when things were much simpler. Made him wish this were that simple, instead of him having to work his way through hidden motives. But this was the closest lodging to where he needed to be and the most private. There hadn't been much of a choice, so he had to work with what he'd been given.

"What made you decide to take on a business such as this?" He decided to draw her out by talking about herself. "It has to be a huge job for one person."

Maggie avoided his gaze by pouring coffee into thick pottery mugs.

"I had this house and a whole lot of empty rooms," she explained. Her pulse quickened as she was drawn back nearly twenty years. "I had a house and a baby and a foster child and needed to support us all."

Nate's fork paused mid-air. "Children? As in plural?"

Maggie smiled thinly. "Yes, for a while I looked after my cousin, until he grew up and did his own thing. He's thirty-one now."

His fork dipped into a slice of peach, but Maggie noticed a pair of creases between his brows. She tried to lighten the mood by cracking a joke. "Now you're doing the math. How old must I be to have an eighteen-year-old daughter and a foster child of thirty-one?"

He swallowed and reached for his water as a snort of mirth bubbled out at her directness, easing the tension. "I guess I am."

"I'll save you the trouble. I'm forty-two. I was

twenty-four when Jennifer was born. Mike was thirteen. He came to me when he was eleven—when I was twenty-two."

She passed him the cream and sugar, then resumed her seat. "And now you want to ask the question and don't know how to do it politely."

Her heart fluttered. Talking about it was hard, and no matter how many times she answered, it never seemed to get any easier. But by now she knew that it was best to get it over with, quick and clean.

Nate had given up all pretense of eating and was watching her closely, so she tried her safest smile. "When I was twenty-five, my husband, Jennifer's dad, was killed in a work accident."

"I'm so sorry."

"It was a long time ago."

Conversation halted. Probing the topic further would be presumptuous, which was part of the reason why Maggie tended to get it over with as soon as possible. Once it was out there, most dropped the subject, uncomfortable with the idea of asking how it had happened, or worse, why she hadn't married again. She knew her reasons. That was enough.

Nate put a bite of pastry and ice cream in his mouth. Her answers had been plain at best, and he knew she was skimming the surface, evading deeper responses. It would be rude to press further. And how much did he really want to know? He was here for a short time. It would be best if he stayed out of her way as much as possible, kept her questions to a minimum. Get the answers he needed and no more.

Besides, there were some questions about his life he wouldn't want to answer. If she wanted to keep her life private, that was fine by him. What he needed from her had nothing to do with her private life beyond Jennifer's —and her—involvement.

The candle at the centre of the table flickered and he watched the flame dance.

Maggie sipped her coffee and changed the subject. "So what brings you to backroads Alberta? Most would choose a more touristy area. Like Banff, or somewhere south of the border. Montana or Colorado. There's nothing around here besides snow and prairie and a bunch of ranches mixed in with the gas industry."

"If this is your tourism pitch, I can see why your beds are empty," he joked.

"This isn't our big season," she answered. "Like I said, most would head to the mountains for the skiing and richer comforts. We get most of our traffic in the summer."

"I'm surprised you don't vacation in the winter, then," Nate suggested.

When she didn't answer right away, he peered closer at her face and it struck him. "You *do* usually travel, don't you? Is my being here…" He paused, knew he was right by the uncomfortable way her gaze evaded his. "You cancelled plans because I was coming." He hadn't thought of that. Hadn't thought of anything beyond doing this assignment, and then dealing with the details.

She shook her head. "It's no bother. I hadn't even booked anything yet."

"But you were going to," he confirmed.

Maggie looked up at him and he was struck again by how young she looked. If he didn't know better, he'd have thought they were close to the same age.

"Mexico isn't going anywhere." She smiled shyly, and their gazes caught.

She tried to cover the moment with her own question. "How long have you been a marshal?"

"Five years. Before that I was in the Marines."

"Oh."

He grinned at her. "And now *you're* trying to do the math. I'll save you the trouble. I'm thirty-three."

"And you like it?"

"I couldn't do it otherwise."

Somehow their voices had softened in the candlelight, taking on an intimacy that surprised him, pleasantly. He watched as Maggie bit the inside of her lower lip and released it. She had a beautiful mouth. A mouth made for kissing.

When he lifted his gaze she was watching him, and her expression was fascination mixed with shock that he'd been staring at her lips.

Attraction, he realized. It had been a long time since he'd felt it. But there was definitely a familiar surge in his blood as his eyes locked with Maggie's, blocking out the muted sound of the television coming from the den. Maggie Taylor raised his temperature, and he couldn't for the life of him understand why.

It was a complication he didn't need. All he really wanted to do was what he'd been sent here to do. He put on a good face; pretended this was just a vacation for some relaxation, but he wouldn't have chosen this for a holiday. His idea of fun wasn't in the middle of some godforsaken Canadian prairie at a bed and breakfast. He certainly hadn't expected to feel whatever it was he was feeling for the proprietress. He wasn't sure if the desire to flirt with her was a detriment or a bonus.

The light from the candles sputtered, throwing shadows on her face. She was as different from his regular type as sun was from rain. Subdued, polite, grounded, yet anything but boring. It took a woman of character and stamina to lose a husband so young and still bring up a family and run a business. How had she done it all alone?

Jen coughed in the den and Maggie looked away as the moment ended. Nate caught his breath as the colour bloomed in her cheeks. He hadn't imagined it, then.

"Excuse me, I should clean this up." Her voice was over-bright as she scrambled up from the table, knocking over her empty mug.

It crashed to the floor, breaking into three distinct pieces.

"Oh, how clumsy of me!" Without looking at him, she knelt to the floor to pick up the pieces. Nate watched, amused. It had been a long time since he'd met a woman who intrigued him, and even longer since he'd had the power to fluster one the way Maggie seemed to be right now.

"Let me help you," he suggested, pushing out of his chair and squatting down beside her.

"Ow!"

Maggie sat back, one of the pieces of pottery in her left hand and a small shard sticking out of a finger on the opposite hand. A drop of blood formed around the tip.

"Maggie, take a breath." Nate took her hand gently in his. "Are you sure coffee was a good idea?" He chuckled as he concentrated on her finger, pinching the fragment between his thumb and forefinger. "Perhaps decaf next time, hmmm?"

He pulled out the shard, but it had gone deeper than he expected, and the drop of blood turned into a substantial streak.

"Do you have a first-aid kit?"

Her voice was subdued. "Of course, I do. Under the sink in the bathroom."

He rose and headed for the stairs.

"The one over there. In my living quarters."

He stopped and looked at the closed door leading off the kitchen. She had wrapped a napkin around the finger and stood up, taking the larger pieces of the mug and placing them gently on the table.

"I'll get it," she said.

"No, you sit tight. I will."

Nate changed direction and went through the door, feeling somehow like he was trespassing. This was crazy. Less than six hours here and he was flirting with the owner and wandering around her private living space. He went into the bathroom, surprised by the scent of cinnamon and apples coming from a scented oil dispenser plugged into the wall. Switching on a light, he was bathed in an intimate glow—no blaring bulbs here. Soothing blue and deep red splashes of colour accented the ivory décor. Nate felt very much like he was intruding.

He searched the small vanity cupboard until he found a white box with a red cross on the top. Then shut off the light and went back to the kitchen, where he found Maggie at the sink, the napkin off her finger as she ran it beneath cold water. She lifted it out of the stream and looked at it closely in the soft light from above the sink.

"I think all of it came out," she explained. "What a klutz I am."

"Not at all." Nate sat the kit down on the counter and flipped open the lid. "It's not deep, so you just need a small bandage."

"I can get it, truly."

"You're right-handed, aren't you? Putting it on lefty would be awkward. I've got two capable hands."

Maggie looked down at his fingers holding the bandage. Capable indeed. His hands were wide, with long tapering fingers. She swallowed but held out her finger anyway.

The sound of the paper wrapper tearing off the bandage echoed through the kitchen. Nate stepped closer, anchoring one sticky end and then holding her hand before wrapping the rest around and sticking it to itself. Her heart pounded painfully; she was sure he could hear it as he applied the small wrap.

"All better," he said softly.

"Thank you," she whispered.

He started to pull his hand away, but for a long moment his fingertips stayed on hers. She lifted her eyes to his and found him watching her steadily. Oxygen seemed scarce as she was entranced by his intense eyes, the shape of his lips. Lips that leaned in ever so slightly.

"You're welcome." And he lifted her finger to his lips and kissed the tip.

3

Nate flipped through the channels aimlessly. There really wasn't going to be much to do here in the evenings, especially when the days were still fairly short. At the end of March, this far north, it was full dark early in the evening. Whatever work he did, it would be during the day. It was becoming very clear that after dinner he'd either spend his time here, in the den, or upstairs in his room reading or working online.

He'd rather be upstairs, putting his thoughts together, but on the off chance that Maggie might come in, he stayed.

He had questions, and the answers could get him started in the right direction. Not to mention the fact that he'd enjoyed their little interplay in the kitchen earlier. It had been a long time since he'd indulged in a little harmless flirtation.

Maggie entered with a coffee carafe and mugs on a tray. She put them down on the coffee table. "I thought you might like some coffee," she offered. "I made a fresh pot and promise not to break any more mugs." She smiled tentatively.

The brew smelled wonderful and Nate brushed aside the thought that he'd be up all night if he drank too much of it. He wasn't about to refuse the gesture. If nothing else, it would give him more time with her, and that wasn't a hardship. "That would be wonderful." When she poured the first cup, he nodded to the second. "Are you joining me?"

She smiled. "If you like."

Nate looked up into her eyes. They were warm and friendly with something more. Perhaps a shy invitation, definitely a quiet curiosity. "I would like." He returned her smile. "It's quiet. The company would be nice."

Maggie took her own cup and sat, not on the sofa next to him, but in a nearby chair. Nate was taking up the couch and she was far too aware of him to sit next to him. In the winter months, this room became the family room, and she often snuggled up on the couch with a blanket and a DVD. In season, it was where the guests went to relax.

Normally she didn't socialize with her guests, either. But normally, her guests didn't travel alone at the end of winter. She was accustomed to guests traveling in pairs. A romantic getaway, or a stop on the way somewhere else. Very rarely did she have singles, and when she did, it was nearly always in prime season when they were out exploring the area or the nearby Rockies, or when other guests were present to facilitate conversation.

But Nate was definitely here alone. She'd noticed the absence of a wedding ring at dinner.

"This gives me a chance to pick your brain," he was saying, and she stopped staring at his hands and paid attention. The tingling sensation that he was more than he seemed prickled once more.

"Pick my brain?"

"About things to do while I'm here."

She exhaled slowly. Just tourist information, then. She'd had the uncomfortable feeling after their interchange in the kitchen that he was about to get personal. "Well, there are always day trips into the mountains. I have pamphlets, but there are lots of winter activities there." She crossed her legs, adopting the tour-guide voice she used with guests. "Or a few hours either northeast or south will take you to major cities for shopping, the arts, whatever you want."

"I meant more locally. What I can do with Mountain Haven as my base." Nate put down his cup and leaned forward slightly. He wasn't going to let her off the hook, it seemed.

Maggie swallowed. His voice was deep and a little rough all the time, it rumbled with soft seduction through the room. The remembrance of her finger against his lips rippled through her.

"We're...we're usually closed this time of year. I'm afraid I haven't given it much thought."

"I see." He looked down into his cup, frowning, then took a drink.

"But...I have some personal gear I could loan you." His disappointment in her answer was clear and she instantly regretted being so cool. She punctuated the offer with a soft smile.

"Personal gear?"

Maggie hesitated. She knew that out in the shed she'd find Tom's things—cross-country skis, snowshoes, even his old hockey skates. They'd been out there over fifteen years, and she'd never had the heart to throw them away.

But holding onto them didn't make much sense anymore. For the last several years, she'd nearly forgotten they were even there. If Nate could get some use out of them, why shouldn't he?

"My husband's things. Snowshoes, skis, that sort of thing." She took a sip of hot coffee to cover the tiny waver she heard in her own voice.

The television still chattered in the background, but Nate went very still. She heard nothing beyond the quiet resonance of his voice.

"That not necessary. I can outfit myself, if you can tell me where to shop."

Maggie nodded. "I understand if you're uncomfortable with using Tom's things." What man would truly want the leftovers of a dead man, after all?

"I don't mind at all. I thought maybe you were uncomfortable with it, which I completely understand."

Maggie looked up. Nate was watching her calmly, one ankle crossed over his knee. His lips were unsmiling, but not cold. No, never cold, she realized. She was starting to understand that what she'd mistaken for coolness earlier was just him waiting, accepting. Like he understood far more than he should for someone so young.

And he was young. When she thought about the

numbers, she realized there was much *behind* her and much *ahead* for him. She'd been married, raised a child, knew what to expect from life and had accepted it. But he had so much yet to discover. She was good at reading people, doing what she did, and unless she missed her guess, Nate had all those things yet to come.

But when she looked into his eyes like she was now, the numbers faded away into nothingness. Somehow, without knowing each other hardly at all, she got the feeling they were strangely coming from a similar place. Like she recognized something in him though they'd never met before. Something that superseded the difference in their ages.

"It's not doing anyone any good in storage. You are most welcome to it."

"In that case, thanks. I appreciate it, Maggie."

He used her given name again and it felt very personal. Like they'd crossed a threshold moving them from simple guest/proprietor relationship to something more. Which was ridiculous, wasn't it?

Maggie leaned ahead and poured herself more coffee. It was good Nate was going to use the things. Letting go of Tom had taken a long time. But the sense of loss never left her completely. Or the sense of regret. She had a box of small trinkets, mementos of those she'd loved, tucked away in a box in her closet. She had memories and other reminders of Tom; the skis and snowshoes wouldn't be missed. It was a long time ago and, in most respects, she'd moved on.

And in the others…that was none of his business.

Jennifer popped in the door, grinning first at Nate and then over at Maggie. "I thought I smelled coffee."

Maggie was glad of the interruption. "You'll have to grab a mug from the kitchen."

With a flashy smile, Jen saluted and disappeared. Maggie couldn't repress the smirk that twisted her lips. Nate looked over at her with raised eyebrows, and Maggie let out a soft laugh. For all of her troubles, Jen was the breath of fresh air that brightened the house when she was home.

"She's got lots of energy." Nate commented dryly, his hand cradled around his mug as he lifted an eyebrow at Maggie.

"That comes from being eighteen."

"You make it sound like you're in your dotage."

She laughed. "Well, I'm a lot closer than I care to admit."

Nate put down his empty cup and rested his elbows on his knees, linking his hands together. "Believe me, Maggie. You're anything but *too old*."

Maggie's pulse leapt as his eyes locked with hers. Too old for what? For him? She couldn't deny the undercurrents that kept running through their conversation, or the way he'd kissed the tip of her finger. The way she'd caught him staring at her lips. Perhaps flirtation came naturally to him. But she was very out of practice.

"I'm old enough to have a grown daughter to worry about."

Jen popped back in the door and headed straight for the coffee pot, oblivious to the tension in the room. As she poured, she gave her mother the update. "Three loads down, one more to go and my term paper has been emailed to my prof."

"Atta girl." It was a relief for Maggie to turn her attention to Jen and away from Nate's probing glances.

"Hmmph." Jen grumbled as she stirred milk and two heaping teaspoons of sugar into her mug. "Break would have been more fun if I could have gone out instead of being cooped up here writing about the War of 1812."

"What exactly do you do for fun around here?" Nate took a sip of coffee.

Maggie looked at Jen. Maggie's idea of going out for fun wasn't quite the same as Jen's. Maggie preferred for Jen to hang out with girls her own age. Maybe go into Sundre to a movie or something. It was one thing about living in a very small community. Maggie remembered it well. Someone would make a liquor run and everyone would converge on an agreed spot. Most of the time it was harmless, but not always. As they both well knew.

"I, uh…" Jen actually faltered, looking at her mother.

Good, thought Maggie. Perhaps Jen was realizing now that what she'd done was serious. And that it definitely wouldn't seem funny to a cop.

"Um, you know, hang out with other kids and stuff. There's not much to do around here. No place to go other than the store."

"The store?"

Maggie answered the question. "The General Store. Unless you go into Sundre or Olds, it's the only place around to pick up what you need." Maggie looked at

Jen, who was staring into her coffee cup. "I'm afraid kids tend to be at loose ends a lot of the time. It's good that Jen's going to school in Edmonton. There's more there for her to see and do."

Jen's head lifted in surprise and Maggie offered a warm smile. Sure, in her heart she also knew there was potential for Jen to get into much more trouble, and that worried her. But by the same token, there was more to catch Jen's interest and keep her busy. It was just hard not being there to make sure she was making good choices.

Maggie went to pour more coffee and realized the cream was empty.

"If you'll excuse me, I'll be right back."

Nate watched her leave, then casually leaned back on the couch, crossing an ankle over his knee again.

"I get the feeling you and your Mom just had a whole conversation."

Jen looked up, her cheeks pink. "Well...yeah. Maybe. How'd you know?"

Nate chuckled softly, settling back into the cushions. "Ah. I too have a mother. One that saw far more than I ever thought she did."

"My mom sees everything."

Nate purposefully kept his pose relaxed, inviting. It might be his only opportunity. "See now? It sounds like there's a bigger story in there somewhere. You get in some trouble, Jen?"

Her lips thinned and he recognized the stubborn rebellion in her eyes.

"You're a cop. If I did, It would be dumb to tell you, wouldn't it?"

Nate nodded. When she got that obstinate jut to her chin, she looked remarkably like her mother. He couldn't help but smile at the thought. "I can see how you'd think that. But you know, I'm not here to bust you for anything. And sometimes an impartial ear comes in handy."

"Why don't you ask my mom?"

"Because I'm asking you. Because maybe I also became a cop to help people."

Again, Jen stared into her cup, avoiding looking him in the eye. "I got into some trouble with the RCMP last year."

"Doing?"

"I got caught with drugs." Her fingers turned her coffee cup around, avoiding him.

"Were you using?" Nate was careful to voice the question gently, without censure.

"No. I mean, I'd tried a joint or two, I guess. Like everyone else. I thought it was gross. I was just…I didn't sell it or anything."

"You weren't using and you weren't selling. Delivery?"

"Yeah, I guess you could say that." Her eyes slid up to his and he knew he'd been right to take it plain and simple. Her fingers stopped fiddling with the mug.

"You were a go-between. And you got caught with it."

She nodded. "Yes. I mean….I know it was wrong, but it was only pot, and heck, it's legal now. My mom was so mad, though. I was…scared to say much of anything, but in the end she made it okay. She made it so I could come home. And then she sent me away to school. A change of scenery, she said."

But Nate knew that tone of voice. He could tell Jen resented being sent away. But his job wasn't to mend fences between Maggie and Jennifer. He held his breath, listening for any evidence that Maggie was coming back. If only she would stay away another five minutes, he might have what he needed. An ID.

"Jen, who were you doing it for? A boyfriend? Did someone threaten you?"

She shook her head so hard he knew whatever came next would only be a partial truth, if that.

"No. No. Peter was never my boyfriend. He's…he's just the go-to guy, you know? On a Saturday when you can't make it into Sundre to the liquor store, or whatever, you go see Pete, and he sets you up."

Nate gritted his teeth. Small potatoes crime, the kind everyone hated but mostly turned a blind eye to as if it would never affect them. "Booze and recreational drugs?" He forced his voice to remain calm and inviting. Damn. Pete seemed to have changed professions, just like Grant had said. There was no doubt in his mind that the local residents probably considered him the community miscreant, but had no idea of his real past.

If he was indeed the man he'd been sent here to find. More than ever now he had to be sure.

"It started out as something fun, something *exciting*, you know? But then it all changed, and I wasn't sure how to get out. And I was scared to talk to Mom. I knew she'd blow her top about it. In one way…" She blushed. "I guess in a way I'm glad I got caught. Because then it was over and done with. I just hate that I disappointed her."

Suddenly Jen's face changed, no longer embarrassed but fearful. "You're not going to say anything, are you? I mean…gosh, I probably said too much… we just sort of got to a place where we're okay, you know? Not fighting about it all the time."

Nate felt guilt spiral through him. He'd actually inspired her trust and now he was indeed going to use what she'd told him. The only thing that made it okay was knowing that in the big picture he was doing the right thing. He had no desire to hurt Jen, or Maggie. On the contrary.

"It's okay, Jen. I wouldn't use what you told me against you."

"You're sure?"

"I'm sure. Like I said, my job is also to help people." *Helping people by getting rid of scum,* he reminded himself. *Helping people by getting the information right.*

"Yeah, and besides, you're from the States. So there's no jurisdiction, right?"

He swallowed. It didn't matter how long he did this; some things simply didn't sit right even when they were necessary. He reminded himself of the bigger purpose and lied. "Yeah, that's right."

"My mom…she was mad, but I think she was more upset that maybe I was in big trouble. I…I don't want to hurt my mom again."

Nate smiled. Jen was a good kid, no matter how

much trouble she'd gotten into. He hoped Maggie knew it. It spoke well of her that she was concerned about her mom's feelings. But his concern was Pete.

"How old is this Pete? I mean, does he usually use young girls to move his stuff?"

"I dunno. Old. Like in his forties, I guess. He just moved here a few years ago. He, you know. Tries to keep it on the low. He's not really hurting anybody. It's just parties and stuff."

Nate hid another smile at Jen's perspective of "old". At eighteen, he supposed it seemed that way. Yet Maggie fell into that bracket and he wouldn't consider her old at all. He remembered the sound of her breath catching in her throat when he'd kissed the tip of her finger. No, there was nothing old about Maggie.

He heard a door shut down the hall and he realized whatever information he'd received was all he'd get. But it was enough.

"Hey, Jen, you want some friendly advice?"

"I guess."

"Make sure you always learn from your mistakes. I can tell that the experience isn't something you'd care to repeat. Take your lessons learned with you."

Take your own advice, buddy, a voice inside him said.

"You're not going to tell my mom? That I told you?"

"Not unless she asks. And you know, she might be really glad to know what you just said. About not wanting to hurt her. Might be a good way to mend some fences."

"I'll think about it."

When Maggie came back in, she put down the

cream and ruffled Jen's hair. "I put your last load in the dryer for you. And hung up your sweater."

"Thanks."

Nate tasted cold coffee and suddenly knew what had been plaguing him for the last few weeks. He was homesick. He was missing someone being there for him when he got in trouble, the way Maggie was there for Jennifer. Someone who cared enough to do the little things, for no reason at all. And despite how complicated the trip was rapidly becoming, he was glad he'd somehow ended up at Mountain Haven.

———

MAGGIE BREATHED ON HER FINGERS, FUMBLED WITH THE key, and finally got it shoved in the lock.

It turned hard, stiff from the cold and lack of use, but finally the padlock sprung apart and she opened the shed door with a flourish.

"Enter, if you dare."

She aimed a bright smile up at Nate. He'd been quiet last night after she'd come back in the room and had excused himself soon after. But this morning he was back to what she assumed was his friendly self. Now he was with her, ready to dig out Tom's things and see if they were fit for use.

He smiled back, his even teeth flashing white in the frosty air. "I don't think I mentioned that I was also a Marine. I'm not afraid of an itty-bitty shed."

"Not even of spiders?"

He laughed. "It's minus a million out here. If they can get through this parka, they deserve a meal."

He ducked into the shed while Maggie waited just outside the door. His sense of humour was a surprise, but it wasn't unwelcome.

"You find anything?" Her breath came out in puffy clouds as she called in after him.

"Yeah. Hang on." A few things rattled and banged as he rearranged articles, pulling things free. Maggie caught a glimpse of his backside as he bent to pick something up from the floor. She stepped away from the door. He was becoming far too alluring and she had to keep her head.

"Incoming!"

She sidestepped quickly as a pair of snowshoes came flying out. When he emerged, cobwebs clung to his coat and hat. She resisted the temptation to reach up and brush them away. Touching him would be a big no-no. She was at least self-aware enough to understand that much.

He proudly held a pair of cross-country skis in one hand and the poles in the other.

"Did you find the boots?"

"Hang on." He pitched the skis in the snow and went back inside, returning with a dusty pair of black boots with square toes. "Size eleven and a half. Should fit all right, even if I double my socks."

"You're crazy to want to go out in this cold." He wouldn't know where he was going, and she knew she'd worry in this weather. "With the windchill it's nearly minus thirty."

"Bracing, wouldn't you say?"

"More like frostbite."

"Yes, but then I'll be out of your hair."

Maggie's lips twitched. "Guests at Mountain Haven Bed and Breakfast are *never* in my hair."

"You say that now, but I'm god-awful when I'm bored. Disposition of a gator."

Maggie laughed and folded her mittened hands as he tried sliding his feet into the snowshoe harnesses. Despite her words, it would be easier for her if he weren't around twenty-four-seven. No matter what should be, the two of them alone in the house held a certain degree of intimacy. Intimacy she didn't want or understand. It had never happened with a guest before, but she could feel it stirring between them. Amicability. The feeling that perhaps they were similar sorts of people. And yes, a level of physical attraction that couldn't be ignored.

"I can't seem to get this on right."

Maggie watched him struggle for a minute, then went to him and knelt in the snow, showing him how to fit his boots into the harness and buckle up the ends.

As she knelt, he bent to see what she was doing, and Maggie felt the heat from his body blocking the wind. He was too close. She fumbled with the straps, so took off her mittens to buckle them with her bare hands. Touching him in any way was a mistake. Each time they were together the ridiculous urges grew. He was big and strong, and she'd already seen glimpses of compassion and humour. How was she supposed to stay immune to that?

"Try that." She went to get up, and immediately felt the pressure of his hand at her elbow, helping her.

She stepped away.

He took a few steps, gained confidence, picked up the pace, and promptly fell.

Maggie giggled into the wool of her mittens; she couldn't help it. One side of his body, from jeans to the side of his toque, was covered in snow.

"You need some help, tough guy?"

"Not from a scrawny thing like you." He planted his hands and hopped up. "Go ahead and laugh. I bet you couldn't do it."

Maggie's snickers died away as he tried again, the gait awkward but steady. He didn't look back so couldn't see the look on her face, see how his casually tossed out words hurt her.

But the truth was she could do it. She used to snow-shoe a lot. First, she'd taught Mike when he'd lived with her in Sundre. Then she'd met Tom and she'd gotten pregnant, and they'd married and moved here. That first winter they'd gone on long jaunts with Mike, and Jen in a baby backpack.

She turned away, closing the shed door and putting the lock back on it. She hadn't realized what she'd had and had squandered so much time asking what if. By the time the truth hit her, Tom was gone, and she was left alone again. Only this time with the responsibility of a teenage foster child and a baby.

Nate jogged back to her, leaving gigantic bird-shaped tracks behind him in the snow. "Thanks for this. It's going to be fun wandering around."

"You're welcome. You can leave the skis and stuff on the porch and bring the boots inside."

"Maggie?"

She looked up at him. His green-blue eyes pierced her. "Are you sure you're okay with me using these? You're quiet all of a sudden. I don't want to intrude, really."

"It's not that. They're not doing anyone any good locked up in there. Don't worry about it." She tried to muster a cheerful smile. "I'm going to make a light lunch before I have to take Jen to the bus station."

"You're going to miss her." His voice was quiet in the winter stillness.

"Yeah. I am. Even though we fight like cats and dogs. Still…I think she's better off where she is."

She knew Jen was. The last thing she needed was being back home all the time. She'd get bored and want to go out with friends and get mixed up with the wrong people again. Maggie had been able to bail her out last time. That wouldn't work again. As lonely as it was without her, she knew she'd made the right decision, getting her into a school there.

"Anyway, she's got to go back so I'm going to do the proper mother thing and ply her with food and a care package." She tried a smile, but it fell completely flat.

Nate bent to take off the snowshoes. "You might not think she appreciates it now, but she does. And once she's grown up, she might even tell you about it."

Maggie had her doubts. "Are you close with your parents?"

She grabbed the skis and poles while Nate carried

the snowshoes and boots and they walked slowly to the house.

"Yes, I am. I have a brother and a sister who chose nice, safe professions, and me, who picked the military and then law enforcement. I know my Mom worries. But you know, even when I was overseas, she still sent care packages. The one thing about living in Florida and having them up north is not seeing them as often as I'd like."

"It sounds as though you had a perfect childhood."

"I suppose, although I'd probably just call it normal."

Maggie swallowed. Nate would never understand *her* life. He'd had brothers and sisters and two parents, and he still had them. This whole family system in place, even if they were miles apart. The only family she had now was Mike and Jen.

"What about you, Maggie? Where are your parents?"

Maggie climbed the steps to the verandah and leaned the skis against the wall. She put her hand on the doorknob but paused, knowing he was behind her waiting for an answer.

"In a plot next to my husband," she replied tonelessly, before turning the knob and going inside.

4

The restaurant was nearly empty, and when Maggie walked in she was surprised to see Nate sitting at a table with Grant Simms. She caught her breath and held it for a moment. Grant wasn't a bad sort; he just *knew* things. Things she would rather Nate not find out.

She wondered briefly why they were together, but then realized it was natural that enforcement types would gravitate to each other. Nate had probably seen Grant come in and looked for some company. Lord knew she wasn't the best conversationalist today.

Nate turned towards the door as she came in and his eyes shuttered, the intimate look warming her. She smiled back despite her misgivings. There was a magnetism—a pull—that she would never admit aloud but couldn't deny to herself. A feeling so unexpected, unfamiliar in its long absence. She couldn't bring herself to feel sorry about the attraction rising up now. It provided a welcome distraction. The alternative was going home to an empty, quiet house. A reminder of how lonely she was when Jen was gone. A taste of how it would be when Jen moved on with her own life and Maggie would be left alone.

She pulled off her gloves and approached the table.

"Jen get off okay?"

"Yes, the bus is gone." His words brought her firmly out of the moment and back to the very real present. She nearly choked on her reply, swallowed against the sudden tightening in her throat as she said the word "gone." Saying goodbye had been emotional to put it lightly. She hated watching Jen go away, hated the helpless feeling that flooded her every time she left. Hated the fear that somehow this could be the last time. In her head she knew it was irrational, but her heart didn't quite get it. Knowing Jen was out of her sight frightened her more than she'd ever admit.

But she said nothing, because Nate didn't need to know, and besides, he wasn't alone. Her eyes skittered to his companion.

His gaze followed hers and he performed introductions. "Maggie, this is Grant Simms."

"Constable Simms." She held out her hand, surprised when the man rose politely and took it.

"Nice to see you, Maggie. Nate tells me you're treating him well."

"Well, as the only guest, I don't have to play favourites, it's true."

"You know each other." Nate looked from one to the other.

"It's a small town, Nate." Grant laughed lightly, but it sounded false to Maggie.

Maggie forced the smile to remain on her lips. In another time she might have liked Grant. He was in his mid-forties, handsome in a crisp, efficient sort of way. But last summer when they'd met it had been in less pleasant circumstances that she'd rather forget. She commented out of politeness only.

"And now you two have met."

"Grant and I attended a conference in Toronto together a few years ago," Nate explained. "We've been catching up."

The two men exchanged a look. Maggie narrowed her eyes. They knew each other before today, then. It was just a crazy coincidence that they'd met up here. How much had Grant told him about her, about Jen? What would Nate think?

Grant Simms was part of the reason why Maggie had been so persistent in Jen going away to school. She knew she should feel gratitude. Things could have been so much worse. But today of all days, it was a bitter reminder of how much she missed the girl she'd known; how far apart she and Jen had grown that it had come to this. Regrets.

A waitress appeared, bearing a coffee pot. "Sit down, Maggie," Nate invited. "Have a coffee."

She didn't see a way to properly refuse, besides, she was suddenly feeling quite raw. She took the chair Nate held out, sat gratefully.

"Cream?"

He held out the saucer containing tiny plastic cups of creamer. She took two, biting her lip as her fingers began to tremble.

The waitress filled her mug while she struggled with the tab on the creamer. It finally peeled back, but by this time her hands were shaking so badly she jostled the cup as she went to pour, sloshing coffee over the edge and on to the table, staining the cloth.

"Oh, how clumsy of me!" She blinked furiously, out of humiliation and sheer emotion. Why couldn't this get any easier? It should get better each time. Instead, it was always the same. She functioned through goodbye and then fell spectacularly apart later. Why couldn't she have made it another hour so she could do it in private, instead of in front of the two men she'd least want to witness it?

"It's okay, Maggie. I've got it." Nate dabbed at the spilled coffee, making her feel even more foolish.

She tried to catch her breath. It would be fine. Jen's bus would drive into Edmonton and she'd go back to campus and her dorm room and in two months she'd be home for summer break. They'd get back to how things were. They could do it, she knew it in her heart. She'd seen glimpses of it today. Her fears were groundless.

Only they weren't. Silly, perhaps, but not groundless. Life could change on a dime.

"Are you okay?"

Nate's voice murmured into her ear, low enough that no one could hear. His warm breath tickled the hair behind her earlobe, and she focused on inhaling and exhaling. When she opened her eyes, Grant had gone to see the waitress about a towel and fresh coffee.

Maggie looked at Simms's retreating back and then up into Nate's concerned eyes. She wished he didn't see so much; it made her feel naked. "I'm fine. I just want to go home, if that's all right with you."

Nate dug in his wallet and dropped a bill on the table as Grant came back with a tea towel in his hand. "Grant, I think we're going to be off. It was nice to see you again." He held out his hand and the other officer shook it.

"Give me a call while you're around, Nate. We should shoot some pool or something."

"Will do. See you later."

"Nice to see you, Maggie."

He was friendly looking and polite but there was something in the other man's eyes she didn't quite trust. He knew. Had he shared that information with Nate after all?

Her response came out frosty. "You, too." She felt Nate's hand, warm and reassuring against her back. She tipped her lips up in a perfunctory smile.

"Let's go, then."

They were almost to the truck when Nate's rough voice stopped her progress. "Hey, Maggie? Why don't you let me drive back?"

She stopped and turned. He'd pulled his collar up in an attempt to keep some warmth close to his ears, but they turned pink in the frigid air. She wished again that she didn't find him so attractive, especially now when she knew she was raw and vulnerable. His clipped hair, straight bearing, and sheer size didn't intimidate her, not at all. She was drawn to it. It was the oddest thing. She'd never gone for the clean-cut, military type before. There was something about them she didn't trust. Whether it was because of past history or simply knowing how dangerous their lives were, Maggie had never gravitated towards that type of man.

But with Nate, even after a few short hours, there was a constant curiosity that took her by surprise. Knowing there was much more to him than met the eye and wondering what it could be; wanting to dig below the surface to find out what mattered to Nate Griffith.

"You want to drive my old beater? Why?"

He laughed, the masculine sound turning her knees to jelly. He had a strong, rich laugh, one that rippled. "I'd hardly call it a beater. But…sorry, it's a guy thing. I feel kind of weird having you chauffeur me around."

"It's okay. Consider it part of the vacation treatment." It was tempting to let him drive. Her hands were still shaking, and she was thankful he'd gotten her out of the restaurant so quickly. But over the years she'd handled everything thrown her way on her own. Knew she could. It was the one thing she was sure of. The last thing she needed was to let him see how fragile she was. "I can drive."

He stopped her at the driver's side door. "Please, Maggie. You were trembling in there." His hands turned her gently so she was facing him, blocked from the wind by his massive body. "Saying goodbye to Jennifer didn't go well, did it?"

He was hard to resist when he looked down at her with obvious concern. When was the last time anyone had been concerned about her? The relief of it was almost enough to make her want to sag against his body and let him carry a little of the burden. But that was ridiculous. He was a virtual stranger.

"It never does. It's just a parent's worry."

"Worry to the point of shaking, and turning white as a sheet?"

She swallowed. She hadn't realized it was that obvious. Somehow saying goodbye set off a reaction every time, but she hadn't realized it showed so very much. She got the feeling he'd keep up the inquisition, and she tried a plain answer, hoping it would stop him from prying more.

"I've lost a lot of people in my life, Nate. Sometimes it hits even though it's been a long time. Saying goodbye…" She took a big breath. Met his eyes and said it all at once. "Saying goodbye triggers a lot of those old feelings of panic. It'll pass. It always does."

"Then you worry about decompressing and I'll worry about the road. This once." He held out his hand, unsmiling, simply waiting.

She took the keys from her pocket and placed them into his hand. He was steady, she already got that. His warm fingers closed over hers.

"Maggie, she'll be fine. She's a good kid."

Grant must have kept quiet, then. Nate wouldn't have said such a thing if he knew about her arrest last year. A tiny sliver of relief threaded through her.

They got in the truck and he started the ignition. Maggie reached over and cranked up the heater, trying to halt the chills that wouldn't seem to stop shaking her body.

"You want to talk about it, Maggie?" He pulled out

of the parking lot, watching her from the corner of his eye.

Her smile wavered a little. Did she? Perhaps. Maybe it would be nice to talk to someone who didn't know everything, who didn't look at her like *that widow who never remarried*. Too many people here knew her past. But she'd kept it all inside for so long she wasn't comfortable delving too deeply.

"I'm fine. It's just..." Her eyes held his as he waited before putting the truck in gear. "I can't protect her when she's away. But she's eighteen. It's right for her to be where she is."

"All moms worry. It's part of the job description." Nate smiled again and she felt it spread over her. He turned on to the highway, leaning back in the seat and resting a hand comfortably on the steering wheel. "But I get the feeling there's more to it than that."

Maggie stared out the window. Her relationship with Jen was so complicated. It had been easier when Jennifer had been small, and life had been simple. But Jen had grown up, wanted her independence. Didn't understand Maggie's need to keep her sheltered and fought her every step of the way. Without understanding that, she didn't think he could understand how much a simple hug of farewell and "I love you" meant. She didn't have anyone to talk to about it and appreciated the impartial ear.

"Jen and I don't often see eye to eye. But today... today was different."

"How so?"

"I didn't get the level of hostility I normally do. We

talked about summer vacation. It was…nice. But it felt…"

The sense of panic settled in her gut again and she pursed her lips.

"It felt?"

She was glad his eyes were on the road so he didn't see the tears flickering on her lashes. "It felt like goodbye. Like making peace. And it scared the hell out of me."

She sighed when he didn't answer. "I know. It's a fatalistic approach and it sucks."

He laughed. "Well, you're very self-aware."

Tension drained out of her at the sound of his chuckle. Telling him had been good. She'd stopped confiding in her friends long ago. The last thing she wanted to do was bore them to tears about the fears that never quite went away. She'd picked up her life and made something of it. She had a successful business, was a mother. It didn't make sense to most of them that she still had issues. Besides, she wanted people to forget about Jen's troubles, and talking about it wouldn't help at all. But Nate was safe. In the overall scheme of things, it would be forgotten soon enough, when he was gone.

"I'm hungry. Let's stop at the store."

"The store?"

"Up here." She pointed to the turn-off. "I'll pick up something special for dinner."

"You got it." He followed her directions, pulling into a parking space and killing the engine.

Nate hopped out of the cab and trotted over to her

side before she could blink. He opened her door and she slid out, self-conscious at his solicitude.

They stood there for long seconds. Nate's heart thudded erratically at the continued closeness, the same feeling he'd had this morning when she'd kneeled to strap on the snowshoes. She'd trusted him today, and lately trust had been in short supply. The more he talked with her the more he realized it couldn't have been easy. Not for a self-sufficient woman like her. As the pieces started to come together, he could understand how putting her kid on a bus today was a big event.

"Nate, I…" she paused, looking up at him. Her eyes were blue, the colour of the Atlantic on a clear day and her lips were parted as she paused, seeming to search for words. For a fleeting second, he thought about putting his lips against hers just to see what would happen. If the need he felt stirring for her was real or imagined. If the warmth of her mouth would take away some of his own misgivings, as well as appease some of her own.

But that would hardly be fair, so he waited for her to finish what she was saying.

The silence drew out, until he prompted her with "You…"

She blinked slowly. He wasn't imagining it, then. There *was* some sort of a connection between them. It hadn't just been the candlelight at dinner last night.

She cleared her throat. "I was just going to ask if you'd like to watch a movie later. We could get snacks for that."

If he were home he'd work out or read or flip through tv channels much as he had last night. It was different now. They would need something to fill the time. To keep him from thinking about how pretty she looked or how she kept him from feeling lonely. They would be alone together. It would be getting dark, there would be dinner with just the two of them and a long evening stretching before them. They'd only be fooling themselves now, insisting it was a hostess-guest relationship. Something more had been forged between them today. A movie would be just the thing to quell the silly urge to spend the evening with her in his arms.

"That might be nice."

She let out a breath, the air forming a cloud above her head. She had to move soon, or he'd reconsider kissing her. Which would be a huge mistake, especially in front of the only store in the community with everyone watching. Even he understood about gossip in small towns. More than she realized. He'd pretended to be surprised she knew Grant, but he wasn't, not at all. He knew all about their past association. How could he, in all conscience, kiss a woman he'd lied to less than an hour before?

"Maggie?"

"Yes?" She shoved her hands into her pockets.

"What's for dinner?"

She smiled at him then and he suddenly realized he'd been waiting for it. Maggie smiling sucked all the bitterness out of the cold air and replaced it with something else. He felt better than he had in a long time, and rather than analyze it to death, the shoulds or shouldn'ts, he simply enjoyed it.

"Come inside and we'll find out," she suggested

impishly, darting for the door, her dark hair streaming out behind her in the wind.

Movie be damned. Nate was starting to realize it would take more than sitting in front of a television to keep him from thinking about Maggie Taylor.

Nate followed her into the store, more intrigued than he remembered being in a long time. He'd sensed a lot of things about Maggie since arriving, but a sense of fun wasn't one of them. Especially this afternoon when she'd nearly come undone in front of Grant. Yet watching her eyes twinkle at him as she flicked her hair out of her face, he realized there was more to Maggie than met the eye. Much more. He was beginning to regret not kissing her when he'd had the chance.

"Hey, Nate, you helping here or what?"

He straightened, pinning a smile on his face. "Helping with what?"

"Dinner. You pick it, I cook it."

She was standing at the meat counter. He went up beside her and noticed she was quite serious about choosing choice cuts. "Steak?"

"Yeah." The corners of her lips flickered in teasing. "You cave man. Like red meat, yah?"

He couldn't stop the snort, surprising both of them. "Yah, red meat good."

"T-bones or rib eyes?"

The very thought had his mouth watering. He was used to cooking for himself, pointless as it seemed. It had been a long time since any woman had taken care making him a meal. To be given the choice…

"Rib eyes. And mushrooms."

She ordered the steaks, adding in a good-sized portion of stewing beef for another meal.

"Any other requests?"

She turned with the paper packages in her hands and he swallowed. She was making an effort, he realized. To dispel the gloom from the start of the afternoon and replace it with something bright and shiny.

"I trust your culinary judgment completely. Surprise me."

She started down another aisle but turned her head at the last moment. "I just might, Nate. I just might."

He had no doubt about it.

5

It seemed changed somehow.

The house actually felt different with Jen gone. Her presence had been a barrier between Maggie and Nate in one way and brought them together in another. Now, with just the two of them at Mountain Haven, the opposite was true. Her absence was forcing them together physically, but propriety reared its head again and Maggie tried to keep things how they were supposed to be. She'd said enough this afternoon when Nate had invited her confidence. It really wouldn't be wise to smudge the lines any further, no matter how empty the house felt with Jen gone. No matter how tempting Nate's company could be.

She opened the oven and pulled out the cookie sheet, placing it on the stove and turning the roasted potatoes so they'd brown evenly. She was a hostess cooking dinner for a paying guest. That was all.

Then why, oh why, did it feel like a date, for heaven's sake?

She paused, the spatula frozen mid-turn. *Because after only two days she'd allowed him in.* She'd broken her own personal rule about becoming friends with guests and had told him personal things that had been incredibly painful to verbalize. It had felt good to talk, and she'd needed it, but Maggie knew it couldn't happen again. She couldn't let herself become vulnerable to him. To anyone.

She slid the pan back in the oven and turned her attention to the Caesar salad. Cooking soothed her, warmed her soul. It was more than nourishment, always had been. She'd learned to cook at her mother's elbow at a young age, and when she'd been orphaned, it had been the one task that gave her any sense of comfort, of connection. It still did.

Nate came to the door and she wondered, in a moment of sheer fantasy, what it would be like if he came up behind her and slid his arms around her waist. To feel the comfort tangibly from his touch, more than the pressure of his hand on hers as he took her keys, like this afternoon. He looked like he'd perhaps taken advantage of the time to have a nap. His cotton shirt was wrinkled and his hair, what there was of it, was slightly mussed. There was definitely something to be said for the rumpled look, she thought as her mouth went dry.

"Smells good."

She reached into a jug, pulling out her favourite salad utensils, using dinner preparations as a refuge. Talking out of turn while she was raw and upset was one thing, but she'd had time to pull herself together. It was up to her to set the tone where it ought to be.

"Thanks. I thought we'd eat in the dining room tonight." She held out the salad bowl. "The steaks are almost done, but if you could take this in, I'll be there in a minute."

When she entered the dining room, she was struck yet again by the sense of intimacy. It was the custom for her guests to eat here, but she'd never experienced a feeling of "specialness" to the room before. Now, with Nate present, it looked—felt—changed somehow. Richer, darker, smaller.

It would have been an out-and-out lie to think that the extra effort she put into the meal was completely platonic. She'd wanted to impress him, to do something special. Perhaps because of how nice he'd been to Jen, or because he'd put up with her episode this afternoon and had listened to her troubles. Perhaps because she was tired of being lonely, of going through the motions, and he was a willing ear.

She put down the tray and unloaded the serving bowls. Nate stood at the corner of the table, pouring the merlot she'd uncorked.

"Thank you." She took the glass from his hand when he held it out.

"No, thank you," he murmured. A candle hissed and sputtered before finding its flame once more. "You've outdone yourself, I can tell."

"Nonsense."

He waited until she was seated before taking his own, and she glowed inwardly at the presence of manners.

"This looks wonderful, Maggie." She handed him

the platter, steaks surrounded by herbed and browned potatoes and he helped himself.

"All in the line of duty." She brushed it off with a glib comment.

His hand paused, then put down the platter. He seemed to think for a moment, his lips pursing in a thin line. "I get the feeling you've been doing things in the line of duty for a really long time. Especially after what you told me this afternoon."

She looked away. Was she that transparent? She'd told him little about her life in the greater scheme of things. Just the basic facts. But what he said was true. She'd shut away so much of life, had focused on what she did and bringing up Jen. It was easier than letting her heart get involved again.

"I enjoy what I do." She put him off. Talking about the bed and breakfast was a nice, safe topic.

"When was the last time you did something purely selfish? Just for yourself?"

She couldn't remember, and she was disconcerted that he'd been able to read between the lines so easily.

She made her hands busy by filling his salad bowl. "I love my job, you know. I couldn't do it otherwise. It makes me happy."

"I don't mean your job."

He put his hand over hers, stopping her from fiddling with the salad. "Maggie."

She stalled, caught by the simple touch.

"Whether or not it's your job…thank you. For making me feel at home here."

Maggie looked up. His eyes were completely earnest,

caught somewhere between that blue and hazel-y green colour.

"You're welcome."

His gaze held her captive in the flickering candlelight as he held her hand. "And for trusting me this afternoon. I'd like to think—maybe—that we're becoming friends."

She pulled back. "I don't usually befriend my guests, Nate."

He thought for a moment, then a smile brightened his face, as if he knew that was exactly what she was supposed to say. "Yes, well, I'm special."

She couldn't help the quiver of her lips at his teasing. How was she to answer that? She got the feeling that he was, indeed, special. Different. But to say so wasn't wise.

"Don't let it go to your head. And thank you. For being so kind today. I'm sorry I was all over the map. I don't usually fall apart in front of my patrons."

"You're welcome." He pulled back, buttered his bread, and broke it into crusty pieces as they enjoyed the meal she'd prepared.

"So, anything else I should know about Maggie Taylor?"

She'd hoped that thanking him would put an end to the personal talk, but that wish fluttered away. She wondered if it was the cop in him, the need to ask so many questions. She focused on spearing a lettuce leaf. "I told you anything that's interesting. I'm really very boring."

He laughed, cutting into his steak. "Yeah, right, Maggie. The last word I'd use to describe you is dull."

She picked up her wine and drank to hide her face. Was he serious? Dull is exactly how she'd put it. She'd had the same life for the last decade and a half. Running this business and raising a daughter. Watching middle age creep up on her. Nothing exciting in that.

"What do you want to know, then? How much starch I put in my pillowcases? Do I grow my own herbs?" She tried to make a joke of it.

"Sure, if that's what's important to you."

A smile teased her lips before she straightened once more, the picture of propriety. "I sprinkle, not starch and I grow some of my own herbs, but not all."

"Did that hurt?"

"No, I guess it didn't."

They ate in silence for a few more minutes and then Nate spoke again. "I'm more interested in how you became the person you are now. How you grew up and what made you choose this as your livelihood."

The crisp romaine leaves wilted in her mouth. She swallowed. Damn him. "The life story of Maggie Taylor? Only if you're having trouble sleeping."

"Why do you do that?" Nate pushed away his plate and cradled his goblet. "Why do you diminish who you are, what you do? I wouldn't have asked, Maggie, if I didn't think it was worth knowing."

She flushed. She had no wish to unearth the pain and disappointment she tried to keep buried every day. Or go into the sad and lonely reasons why she'd chosen to open a bed and breakfast. What she'd revealed earlier was all he was getting today. It was time to put a stop to this line of questioning right now, because she was beginning to feel like this was an interrogation, not a heart to heart. Like he wanted her to tell him things she shouldn't. She stood, piling his plate on top of hers. "Do you want dessert? There's pumpkin cake with caramel sauce."

His eyes assessed her; she could feel them burning into her as she cleared the dishes.

"I'm sorry, I'm prying. It's unfair of me."

"Yes, it is. I appreciate your listening to me this afternoon when I was upset. But the details of my life are personal. And I know you will respect that."

"I like you, Maggie. I was simply curious."

She couldn't seem to come up with a response. He stood and gathered what was left of the dirty dishes and followed her into the kitchen, putting them on the empty counter.

"Maggie?"

"What." She put down the dishes and turned to face him. She couldn't do this. Being stuck with someone every hour of the day was for some reason, very difficult. Most who came to Mountain Haven were interested in the area, in *their* lives—not hers. Trouble was, she wanted to tell him. To unload all the pain she'd held inside for so many years. She didn't understand it. Couldn't fathom why he was different. She'd never felt such a compulsion before.

He didn't say anything. He stood not five feet in front of her, but nothing came out of his mouth. She saw the muscles bunch beneath his shirt and she wondered what it would be like to run her fingers over the skin of his arms, of his broad shoulders.

"What," she whispered again, shocked when she heard her voice come out warm and husky, like the caramel sauce she'd made for the cake.

Without warning, he took two steps forward, curled his hand around her head, and kissed her.

His lips were warm and tasted faintly of the acidic richness of the merlot. Taken by surprise, and on the heels of her own thoughts, she didn't push away. Her lashes fluttered down as his arm came around her, tucking her close to his hard body as his lips opened wider, taking the kiss deeper.

And oh, he felt marvelous. Strong and patient and thorough. Her heart pounded, sending the blood rushing through her veins, awakening her. He was vibrant and young and mysterious and so very, very real. Her hands slid over his shoulder blades, down, down, until they encountered the back pockets of his jeans.

He broke the kiss off in stages: gentle, fluttering tiny kisses on the corners of her mouth, making her weak in the knees and wanting more, not less. She chased him with her lips, and he caught her bottom one in his teeth before letting go and putting a few inches between them.

She looked up, frightened by the intensity of his gaze, more frightened that perhaps her own mirrored it so blatantly. It was a shock to realize that she wanted him. Wanted a man she hardly knew. Wanted him in the most basic way a woman could want a man.

Right now she'd crawl into his skin if he'd let her.

She pushed away blindly, stopping only when her backside hit the counter. Her breaths were shallow, ripe with arousal. All from a single kiss, a few fleeting moments where their bodies touched.

"I've wanted to do that all day."

And the words, huskily spoken in the muted light, sent a rush of desire flooding through her.

Shame reddened her cheeks. This was wrong. He was patiently waiting for her reaction and all she could do was feel embarrassed that he'd affected her so strongly. She'd pushed away her sexual being for so long she'd all but forgotten it existed. Had settled for a dim appreciation of a man's looks on occasion. But she'd never, not since Tom, behaved in such a wanton way.

"I…you…pumpkin cake." She stammered and wanted to slide through the floor into oblivion. Any pretense of dignity was gone.

"Not right now."

"C..c..coffee?"

"Maggie. Should I apologize?" His words were soft, with that hint of gravel rumbling through and her pulse leapt at the intimacy of it. "I don't want to."

I don't want you too, either. She raised her chin as best she could. She had to put some distance between them somehow. "It would be appropriate."

Who was she kidding? It wasn't like she hadn't participated willingly. He might have initiated the kiss but she'd been right there, keeping up.

"I'm sorry." His voice was husky-soft in the dim light filtering in from the dining room. "I'm sorry you're so damn pretty I had to kiss you."

Holy hell.

She couldn't do this. Couldn't. "Yes, well, I've known

you two days. You're a guest in my house. A paying guest. Perhaps you should remember that."

It might have worked if her voice hadn't trembled at the end. She gathered what little bit of pride she had left around her and swept from the room.

He wasn't the only one that needed reminding.

————

Sunlight filtered through the window of the bedroom as Nate stirred. He squinted against the bright light, checking his watch. Eight-fifteen. He never slept this late.

He usually didn't lie awake until the wee hours thinking, either. But he had last night.

He rose, pulling on the clothes he'd laid out. Long johns beneath heavy grey-toned camouflaged pants. Thick socks and a long-sleeved shirt under a crew necked cotton pullover. He'd layer today and adjust. He took the backpack out of the bottom of the closet, left in it what he'd need, and stowed the rest in the bottom of his duffle.

A day out of the house was definitely in order.

He'd been foolish to kiss Maggie last night. Problem was, he'd been thinking of it all afternoon and through dinner. He enjoyed seeing her flustered, enjoyed the moments of banter between them. But then, seeing her vulnerable, knowing how difficult she found it watching her daughter leave, brought out his protective side. It was something he'd inherited. He couldn't do what he did without it.

He put the pack on the bed, seeing her sad eyes in his mind. It wasn't all about justice. Most people thought so, and for some it was true. But not for him.

Sometimes it wasn't about punishing the guilty, but protecting the innocent.

He padded down the stairs in his stocking feet and wandered into the kitchen. It was quiet, not a dish or crumb in sight. The appliances gleamed and floor shone. He smiled to himself. He was beginning to recognize her penchant for order, especially when she was preoccupied. Had his kiss done that? Or had it simply been because of Jen?

He frowned as his early morning thoughts trickled back. Had she put all that extra effort into the meal, had she kissed him back, simply as a substitute? To keep herself from thinking about her daughter's absence? Had he been a distraction?

And wouldn't that be a good thing? A harmless flirtation was far more desirable than something complicated. Yet…the thought of him being a stand-in chafed, good idea or not.

Nate wondered if Maggie had had the same trouble sleeping and was making up for it now. Quietly he filled the coffeemaker and started the brew filtering. There was no sense dwelling on it. A more important question was whether or not she had a thermos on hand for him to take with him today.

The side door opened and Maggie appeared, completely dressed, pulling her hair back into a sensible ponytail.

When she looked up at him, his heart gave a solid

thump. Where had that come from? It was difficult enough being here under the present circumstances. Attraction, kissing…they weren't on the agenda. He couldn't afford to be distracted. And she certainly wouldn't understand if she found out the truth. He offered his best, polite-only smile.

"Good morning."

"Good morning," he answered back. Silence fell, awkward. So the kiss wasn't forgotten, nor forgiven. The smile faded from his face. "I started the coffee. I hope that's alright."

"I'm sorry I wasn't up to see to it."

Great. Now they were speaking—and standing—like wooden statues.

"Maggie, I'm sorry about last night. I was out of line. Your business is yours. I had no right to pry."

He sensed her relief as the clouds cleared from her eyes. "Thank you, I appreciate that." She offered a small smile and he watched her go to the cupboard and dig out ingredients. Perhaps his greatest transgression hadn't been the kiss, then, but the intimate questions.

"I like you, Nate. You're a nice guy." He winced. A nice guy? Hardly. Her words were hollow as she spoke from within the cabinet. "It's understandable that things…progressed, I suppose. But I'm not comfortable with it. It can't happen again."

"I know that."

She turned around, flour bin in hand, her smile a little easier. "I'm glad. And I hope you like pancakes."

She couldn't know. Couldn't possibly know how much he wanted to tell her everything. To tell her why he was really there, how it would help her, and Jen. But he couldn't. It was what it was. It was pancakes and pleasantries and half-truths.

"Pancakes are good." He thought of the day ahead. "With a couple of eggs would be even better."

"Eggs I can do. How do you like them?"

"However you fix them will be fine." He offered her the first truly genuine smile of the day. "I'm used to eating them in all forms, believe me."

She beat the batter in the bowl as the griddle heated. "I suppose you have, with your past history. What's your favourite?"

He grinned at her back. "Over-easy."

"Then that's what you'll have. What are your plans for the rest of the day?"

The tension had dispelled with apologies and talks of breakfast. "The temperature's gone up a bit, so I thought I'd give those snowshoes a workout." He went to the counter and took the plates and cutlery she was laying out as the first pancakes sizzled on the pan. "I've been two days without physical activity. Add home cooking to that…"

He put the plates at the kitchen table, turning back as she put the pancakes on the warming tray and cracked eggs into a fry pan.

"There's syrup and juice in the fridge," she called out, pouring two more perfectly round circles on the greased griddle.

It was something he missed, more than he'd realized. Everyday chatter over meal preparations, having someone to sit with at the table. Now it only happened when he was home in Philadelphia for holidays, with his brother and sisters around. Mom cooked for everyone, and ribbing and teasing were the order of the day. He was surprised to find it so far away from his ordinary life.

When the eggs were done, she filled his plate. "Sit down, Nate, and I'll bring you some coffee."

The pancakes were light and fluffy, and he poured syrup—real maple syrup, not the table version—over the top. Two eggs, done to fragile perfection, sat alongside. He'd heard before that the way to a man's heart was through his stomach. As his own rumbled, he thought that just might be true.

"Hey, Maggie?"

"Hmmm?"

"You wouldn't happen to have a thermos, would you? I'd love to take some coffee along this morning."

"I've got one around here somewhere."

She took her place across from him. "How long are you planning on being out?"

"Most of the day, I think."

"Then you'll need a lunch."

"You don't have to…"

"Don't worry about it. It's all part of the 'extras' I quoted your boss."

The pancakes went dry in his mouth. Of course. The tentative friendship they'd forged was punctuated with reminders that he was a client. It was as she'd said all along. This was her job. She was being paid to see to his needs. Food and comfortable shelter.

"Thank you, then."

He sliced through his pancake. He'd asked for the coffee but had planned on a few protein bars keeping him going throughout the day. If the USMS was footing the bill, there was no reason for him not to take the lunch. Maggie had reverted to her pleasant, professional self. It was like the emotions of yesterday hadn't happened. It was for the best.

He pushed out his chair. "Thanks for breakfast. I'll go upstairs and get my pack."

In his room he reconsidered his clothing and stripped off his cotton shirt, putting his vest beneath it. He wasn't anticipating any trouble, but there was no harm in being cautious. Taking care, an ounce of prevention and all that. He checked his pack one last time and went back downstairs.

"Your lunch."

Maggie appeared in the foyer with an insulated pack and a silver thermos. "Sandwiches and fruit. And a slice of the cake you missed last night. I hope that's okay."

"It's perfect." He took them from her and tucked them carefully into his bag, withdrawing his GPS at the same time and tucking it in his parka.

"Are you sure you know where you're going?"

He nodded. "I have a map of the roads right here." He held up the unit. "As long as I stay within the grid, there's no way I'll get lost."

"I'll see you at dinner then."

He pulled his toque over his ears. "Yes, ma'am."

Outside, he squinted in the sunlight and put on his sunglasses. He strapped on the snowshoes bare-handed and pulled on his gloves. It was cold, but not the frigid bitterness of yesterday.

He started off over the lawn, his gait gaining rhythm as he caught his stride. According to his information, a little over two miles south west from here he could set up, dig in, and enjoy more of her coffee as he watched. And waited.

6

Maggie watched him go, heaving a sigh of relief when he crossed through the grove of trees at the edge of her property. She closed her eyes, breathing deeply, willing her body to relax.

This morning had been nothing more than an acting job, and one she wasn't sure she could keep up.

His apology had gone a long way, but as soon as she'd seen him standing there, looking large and dangerous and undeniably sexy, she'd wanted nothing more than to kiss him again and see if it had really been as good as she remembered.

Something had changed. At first it had been a simple appreciation for a good-looking man, full stop. The last person she'd ever be interested in was someone in law enforcement. Maybe the problem was that he wasn't here in any official capacity. He didn't wear a uniform, or a badge, or carry a weapon. It made it easy to forget. Until something intruded to remind her. Like seeing him with Grant Simms. Or the way he questioned her last night.

And then she forgot all over again when he kissed her and turned her knees to jelly.

She went back to the kitchen and began to tidy the mess. Jen had put the idea in her head, but it hadn't taken much to keep it there. And now Jen was gone, and Nate wasn't, and it wasn't right that she should have such feelings. Maybe she'd been wrong not to date all this time, because it felt suspiciously like slaking a thirst. Nate was younger and energetic, and she found that irresistible. And it was foolish to think she could relive her youth through a man who was just passing through.

This morning was a new day and she'd awakened knowing that keeping distance from Nate was the best thing for everyone. The emotional pitch from yesterday had dissipated and she was left with a clearer head. Nate was leaving within a few weeks and she couldn't get attached to him. Anything that happened between them was temporary. They both knew it, and also knew further episodes like last night's would be pointless. After that kiss…even flirting was a dimension best left unexplored. These weeks at Mountain Haven weren't real. What was real was his life back in the States, the one where he was a marshal who spent his days apprehending criminals.

She spent the morning cleaning, discovering with great interest that Nate was a neat lodger. He'd already made up his bed, and his laptop was neatly closed, the mousepad and cordless mouse sitting on top of the cover. There were no clothes laying about. In fact, except for the laptop on the desk, she could hardly tell anyone was even staying in the room.

For some odd reason, she didn't find that knowledge all that comforting.

She curled up with a book in the afternoon. The sun sliding through the south facing window warmed her, making her drowsy. She hadn't slept until nearly two a.m., and after the emotional rollercoaster of yesterday, the six-plus hours she did get hadn't seemed to have alleviated all her exhaustion.

When she woke, it was after four, dinner wasn't started, and Nate wasn't back, despite the darkening shadows of fading daylight. She'd been dreaming, odd dreams with Nate and Jen and Grant. Nothing that made sense. Jen, in handcuffs, with Nate holding her wrists. Grant coming forward and pinning some sort of medal on Nate's chest.

She stood up, rolling her shoulders and dismissing it. It was silly, that was all. She could puzzle it out easy enough. It was worrying that Nate would find out about Jen, and after seeing Grant and saying goodbye yesterday, it was probably natural.

A niggle of concern skittered down her arms as she realized another hour and Nate would be out of daylight. Where could he have gone that would have taken him all day? He had to be exhausted. Had he gotten lost despite his assurances to the contrary?

He'd definitely cooled off when she'd mentioned his boss, too. Knowing she was behind schedule, she put chicken breasts in the microwave to thaw, the sound of the appliance filling the empty house. He hadn't appreciated the work reminder. As soon as she'd brought up the fact that his bill was paid, he'd gone cold and distant. She wondered why that was. Wondered why he'd chosen to come here, of all places. What had forced him to take a leave of absence?

As she kept her hands busy, her mind kept pace. She could understand the leave being paid, but it still didn't quite sit right that his vacation was being paid by the Marshal Service. Not if it were a personal trip.

The sound of his boots on the porch coincided with a sudden thought. She couldn't believe she hadn't thought of it before.

The bill, the location, his contact with Constable Simms.

He was here on a job. It was the only thing that made sense, and an icy spear shot through her body as the door opened.

He stomped inside, cheeks flushed and boots in hand, putting them on the mat so that no snow fell on her floor.

"Sorry I'm late."

Maggie didn't know what to say. She was still reeling from the possibility that had zoomed through her head. What if he had been lying to her all along? What had he really been doing today? How was he connected to the very same constable responsible for Jen's arrest?

And how in the world did she go about getting the truth? Did she even want to know? Really? She took a step backward.

"Maggie, are you okay?" He was across the foyer and in the hall in a flash. "Is it Jen?"

Oh, Lord. She was horrible at poker faces. She'd really have to do better, because if her suspicions were correct, he was a heck of a player.

"No, Jen's fine. I fell asleep this afternoon and I think I'm still waking up." She gave a light laugh, then frowned when it came out with a false ring.

"I'm going to go change. Fell down a few times and got wet." He started for the stairs.

"Nate?"

He paused with his hand on the banister.

The words she wanted didn't come. She wasn't sure she was wily enough to trick him into answering and was afraid of asking point-blank. What if he were here on a job? Would it change anything? Certainly not between them. There was no them.

"Nate, I…"

His fingers gripped the railing tighter and she closed her eyes briefly, taking a fortifying breath.

"I had a lot of time to think today and I was wondering what happened that made you need a leave of absence."

She blurted it out in one rapid sentence before she could think of taking it back.

"Well. That's blunt."

His eyes cooled as he pressed his lips together. He didn't want to talk about it. Either that or he was hiding something. Either way she found she suddenly wanted to hear the answer very much.

"Perhaps my reasons are private." He turned to go back up the stairs, but she persisted.

"But the service is paying all your expenses, and the

first time you go into town I find you talking to local
authorities."

Nate stared at her. She was way too close to hitting
on the truth. Yesterday he'd thought maybe she'd ask
questions after seeing him with Grant, but he realized
she'd merely been wrapped up with Jen. Now that she'd
had time to think, not everything added up nice and
neatly. The way she was looking at him now, it was as
though she knew. But on the off chance she didn't, he
kept his expression carefully neutral.

He took his hand off the banister and stepped off
the landing, putting less distance between them. He
remembered how she'd felt against him last night. Had
thought about it a lot today when the job got boring.
There was a chance, a slim one, that he could divert
her now.

"You want to know why I had to take time off, is that
it?" He made sure he worded it carefully—the reason
for his leave, not the reason for being at Mountain
Haven. He didn't want to have to out-and-out lie again.
He'd rather angle the truth.

Even he knew it was a flimsy distinction.

"I…I do." She folded her hands in front of her. "I
know I'm prying. And I told myself I wasn't going to
ask. But I'm asking anyway."

"Funny. I asked you about your life last night and
you closed up tighter than a clam." He'd been tempted
to tell her the truth earlier this morning, seeing her
warm from her bed, remembering how she'd felt in his
arms last night. Thankfully he'd been smart enough not
to. Because he was beginning to get the picture that she

didn't like cops. First the way she acted around Grant yesterday and the cold way she was looking at him now. He let his gaze drop to her lips. "At least at first."

She blushed at the innuendo but persisted. "I know. But you're a guest in *my* house."

"And when I arrived, you assured me that privacy for your guests was of the utmost importance."

Perhaps if he pushed the topic off track enough, she'd take the bait and move on.

"Perhaps concern for my own safety trumps that."

Dear God, what *had* run through her mind today? He wondered briefly if she'd gone through his things, but to ask would only confirm her suspicions and somehow he knew she wouldn't have done that. No, she'd be honest and ask like she was doing right now. And he had no idea what to give her for an answer.

"Where did you go today, Nate?"

She wasn't going to let it go. And he knew the only way to appease her was to give her the one story he was allowed to give. Even if he absolutely hated retelling it.

"All right. Let me get changed into dry clothes and I promise I'll tell you."

He jogged up the stairs, avoiding her probing gaze. He had to get out of his gear first. The last thing he needed was for Maggie to discover there was more than skin beneath his street clothes.

When he came back down, she was emptying dishes out of the dishwasher.

"Your things," he said quietly, holding out the thermos and bag.

"Thank you."

She put them down and simply waited, her eyes pinning him to the spot.

"Is this about yesterday, Maggie? Because if it is, we can keep this business only. I admitted I crossed a line. We can stop this right here."

Her cheeks flushed slightly. "It's that bad, then. Bad enough you'd try changing the subject a hundred times before talking about it." She turned back to her dirty dishes.

She had him to rights there. There was no pleasure rehashing the past. He'd failed, and it ate at him. Almost as much as being forced to go on leave. He didn't need vacation. He needed to focus.

If he didn't feel the strong need to protect her so much, he'd come out with the truth and be done with it. He hated lies.

"It was a month ago." The words sounded strangled to his ears, so he cleared his throat and started again. "It was a month ago and a case of bad information. We were on assignment. My team. To bring in a sex offender. We knew he had firearms on the premises... that much was correct. So we were...armed accordingly."

He paused and swallowed. How much should he tell her? Enough to appease her, he supposed. And not so much as to give away his reason for being there. Maggie closed the dishwasher door and gave him her full attention. He didn't know what to do with his hands, so he hooked his thumbs in the belt loops of his jeans.

"The plan was to go in after him. When we gather information, it's pretty complete, so we can make the best tactical plan possible. It was all organized, everyone had their job. Only somehow he must have known we were coming. I don't know whether he was tipped or saw us or what, but he met us at the door."

He looked at her briefly. She couldn't know how hard this was for him, to admit his worst moment. As he faced her, the images came back. The ones that had forced his break from work to begin with. Sounds of gunfire, everything moving in slow motion when in reality it all went down in a matter of seconds. The prolonged moment when he saw the results, the picture branded on his memory.

"He fired. We fired back. You have to understand. All our information said that he was home alone, we had no reason not to trust it. But he wasn't. There was a woman. His daughter. She took a round and was killed."

It all came out like an official report. He looked away. "So now you know."

"Did you shoot her?"

He licked his lips. "Me personally? No."

"Then why do you carry the burden?"

Wasn't it enough that she had the truth? Why did she have to keep asking questions? It didn't matter who had pulled the trigger. It had been a fatal error.

"It was my team, Maggie. I was in charge."

"It was a mistake, a tragic mistake."

His hands pulled away from the loops and his fingers tightened. "You don't get it. I can't make mistakes. Would you say the same thing if it had been Jen in her shoes? If it had been your daughter who'd been killed?"

Nate turned and escaped out the door on to the

verandah, into the blessed coolness of winter air. Telling Maggie had only made him angry again. He should have foreseen. There simply wasn't room for that kind of error in his job. Worrying about killing someone, the wrong person, or losing a member of the team far outweighed the feeling of personal danger.

His boss had made the leave non-negotiable, even though all Nate wanted to do was get back in the field. He needed work, not time off to think of all the things he'd done wrong.

Then, the leave had become part of his cover and he resented it. It was over and done with. He'd learned from his mistake. Now he wanted to move on. He sure as hell didn't like—or want—the look of sympathy he'd seen on Maggie's face.

Maggie came out behind him, pulling a shawl over her shoulders. She put a hand on his arm and he pulled away.

"Nate, I'm sorry. I shouldn't have pried."

"Now you know and can stop asking."

She took a step backward at his harsh tone and he hated himself more for hurting her, too. This was exactly why he wished he could just tell her why he was here and forget all the secrecy.

He didn't like lying to Maggie. He could argue with himself and say he hadn't lied, that he'd stretched the truth, but it was the same thing. And the last thing he needed was her pity. But he couldn't tell her his assignment and protect her, too. He knew which was more important.

"Thank you for telling me." Her voice was quietly

apologetic. At least his answers seemed to have satisfied her. As she turned and went back inside, he shook off the guilt at smudging the lines of truth. She'd accepted his story completely, and he'd done his job. As much as he hated it, the truth of his "leave" had satisfied her.

He swallowed, not knowing how to patch things up, knowing they should or else the next several days were going to be torture. He followed her as far as the doorway.

"You've got to understand something, Maggie. This is what I do. I'm a marshal and I do my job and if there are consequences to that, I deal with them."

She turned and faced him for a moment, and the warmth from before vanished. "That's very clear," she murmured. And she walked away from him.

His hand smacked the pillar of the porch in frustration. He hated dishonesty. With a passion. Yet this wasn't about being honest. It was about protection. Protection for her, for himself, for the whole community if it came to that. It was a big picture thing. Shifting the truth shouldn't be a big deal. Maggie was temporary in his life. There wasn't room for feelings.

But as he remembered how her lips had clung to his last night, he felt guilt crawl through him anyway.

Guilt because she was, in a sense, part of the job and all he wanted to do was pull her into his arms again.

Right now, the best thing to do was keep his distance.

———

MAGGIE HEFTED THE GROCERY BAGS IN HER ARMS, balancing them carefully so she could still use her keys to get in the house. It was mid-afternoon; she'd still have time to make the steak and Guinness pie she had planned for dinner. Mealtimes were the only times she saw Nate now. He ate in the morning, took a bagged lunch, and spent the whole day outside. The weather was warming, hovering just below zero, and soon the snow would melt enough that he wouldn't be able to use snowshoes or cross-country skis anymore. He came back tired, ate his dinner, and spent evenings in his room. The few times she'd spoken to him after seven p.m., he'd either been reading or sitting at his laptop.

She'd been wrong to push. She knew it now, had known it as soon as she'd touched his arm and he'd pulled away.

It was good that he was keeping his distance. Because the more she saw him, the more confused she became.

How could the one thing she disliked about him also be the one thing that seemed to attract her? She shook her head even though no one was there to see her. The last thing she wanted was to be involved with someone in law enforcement. Then why did she find it so unbearably sexy? It was just as well their flirting had stopped.

Her key turned easily in the lock; the door was open. She frowned. She was sure she'd locked the deadbolt when she left.

She put the bags down on the porch and eased inside. The first thing she noticed were Nate's big boots on the mat by the door. She exhaled, relieved. It was only Nate, then.

He appeared around the corner and she tried a smile, hoping eventually he'd thaw out and treat her to one of his own and they could reach some level of comfort. "You're back early," she said easily. "So…how did you get in? I suppose doing what you do, you know all the tricks, right? What was it? Credit card? File and pick?"

He held up a hand. "Spare key. You really shouldn't leave it in so obvious a place."

There was something off. She sensed it. He didn't smile, but there wasn't a tone of chastisement in his voice either. It wasn't about where she'd put her key. It was something else.

She shut the door, forgetting the groceries sitting outside. "What is it?"

He came forward and her heart started beating faster, a thread of apprehension skimming over her limbs. Whatever it was didn't look good; his face was tight and drawn.

"Jen called."

It seemed as though her heart tripped over itself as her breath caught and held, strangling her.

"There was a stabbing on campus."

The life went out of Maggie's limbs. She felt the floor coming up to meet her when Nate's arms caught her full weight.

"God, Maggie!"

Her head spun, dizzy. Jen. Jen. Jen.

"Maggie. Snap out of it."

His voice came from far away, swimming in the back of her brain.

"Maggie!"

He gave her a shake and she met his gaze, not quite seeing. "Maggie! She's fine. She's fine."

Maggie nodded dumbly.

"Look at me."

He was on his knees, holding her on his thighs, bracing her with an arm. His free hand cupped her chin, forcing her to look upwards. His eyes, darkened with worry, anchored her. She clung to them as she tried hard to make sense of his words.

"Maggie. Clear your mind," he ordered. Her gaze dropped to his lips. "Think. If she weren't okay, she couldn't have called."

It got through. She nodded, letting out her breath and willing some of the panic to release its grip.

Jen was okay.

"I'm sorry. It was a stupid reaction," she stammered.

"I understand. I didn't mean to scare you." He held her with firm hands, taking her weight.

She became aware of the hardness of his legs beneath her, the tight grip of his hands on her arms. She should pull away, but she still felt so shaky she didn't trust herself to get up. It felt too right, letting him carry the weight for a while. So long since she'd allowed herself to lean on anyone.

He pulled her close, tucking her head beneath his chin and stroking her back soothingly. "I never thought of how you'd react. I should have, knowing your history.

I should have said she was fine first. God, Maggie, you dropped like a rock."

"I feel stupid." His hand was warm and she let herself absorb it, drawing strength from it.

"Don't."

And then she felt it. A smile that she could picture creasing his face, moving against her hair. She closed her eyes, relief sluicing through her, ridiculously happy that he wasn't angry with her anymore. "I thought you were mad at me." He'd hardly spoken to her since the night she'd pried into his past.

"Not at you. Maybe just…angry in general." He kissed her hair lightly and her eyes sprung open. He pushed her away slightly. "Are you all right now?"

She nodded. "I think so."

"I'd meant to tell you that she called because she didn't want you to see it on the news and worry. But you didn't give me a chance."

She pushed out of his arms and stood up, feeling at once the loss of the security found in his arms. "I don't know why I did that."

He hopped up from his crouched position. The last thing she expected from him was gentleness, not after the way things had been strained for several days. His fingers touched her cheek, stroking softly.

"I think you know exactly why it happened. You said yourself, you've suffered a lot of loss. Do you want to talk about it?"

She looked up into his eyes. He'd passed an olive branch and it was up to her whether or not to accept it. But she didn't talk about her past. No one wanted to hear about it. "Let's face it, Nate. My story's a bit of a downer. It's no big deal."

Another smile tugged at the corner of his lips. "You know, that sounds vaguely familiar."

"Touché."

He let her go, but she felt more connected to him than she ever had before, even more than being held in his arms or kissed. "I'll think about it. For right now, I'm going to bring the bags inside and call Jennifer."

"She's a good kid, Maggie. She knows how much you care and worry. If she didn't, she wouldn't have thought to call you."

Tears stung her eyes. How he seemed to know what she needed to hear was uncanny. "Thanks, Nate. That means a lot."

"Anytime."

She turned her back to him so he couldn't see the naked yearning on her face. Jennifer's welfare was such a hot button for her. The best thing she could do now was leave before she bawled all over him, so she started towards the stairs. He had no idea how tempted she was to take him up on his offer.

7

"Maggie. Wait."

"Just leave me alone, Nate. Please. I'm fine." She stopped at the bottom of the stairs, blinking back tears. She wasn't. She was embarrassed, vulnerable, feeling like a fool. Nate kept seeing her falling apart and he kept picking up the pieces. It was becoming a disturbing trend, and one she needed to put to an end. He was, by trade, a protector. He wasn't *her* protector.

She hadn't realized he'd come up behind her until his hand, wide and warm, fell on her shoulder, kneading gently. "I'm the one that saw your face. The one that caught you as you collapsed. You're not okay. You might as well tell me and get it out."

She tried to exhale but the air came out in shaky jolts, the very sound tearing her apart a little more with each breath. She was so tired. Tired of being afraid, tired of pretending. All it did was exhaust her. He put his other hand on her right shoulder, both hands now massaging gently.

The caring touch ripped away any shred of control she had left, and she dropped her head, two tears splashing over her lashes and down her cheeks. She tried to sniff them away but failed miserably.

"Please don't be kind. I can't bear it."

"Why?"

The question was what she needed, something to shift the focus from his hands on her shoulders. She turned to face him, straightening her shoulders. "You want reasons? Let's start with the fact that you're here for a few weeks and then gone again. You're just passing through, Nate, and we both know it. And then... well there's the whole cop thing. You're a marshal first and foremost, as you so eloquently pointed out the other day. Not to mention you're..." she paused, her cheeks flushed as she blurted out, "You're nearly a decade younger than I am!"

The words echoed in the hall. She lowered her voice. "And that's the last thing I need. Or want."

"Did I imply that this was something more?"

She huffed. "Imply? Constantly! Starting with the first night when you kissed my finger!"

She gaped when a smile curled his lips and he leaned against the banister.

"Ah yes. When you grew so flustered you dropped your cup. And you should know I couldn't care less about your age. It's just a damned number." He slid a few inches closer and she instinctively backed up.

"Don't flirt with me, Nate. We're both past it."

His smile faded. "I only wanted to help you and

you're making this my fault. Perhaps you can explain that."

How on earth could she explain that being with him made him feel more vulnerable that she could ever remember being? His profession threatened her. And her attraction for him was equally as frightening. Because she was undeniably attracted to all those things that scared the daylights out of her.

And those fears blended with the hurts of the past and the result was a woman who was incapable making sense of it all and threatened to be overwhelmed. Above all, the urge to let him help was so strong.

"I can't do this. I can't cry all over a guest. And that's what you are, though I seem to keep forgetting it. Please…just let me be."

But he ignored her plea. He captured her hand and pulled. "I think we both know that I'm not just a guest. Not anymore." He tugged again, pulling her into the strong circle of his arms.

Oh, the warmth of him, the smell…her own laundry soap blended with his aftershave and that little bit of something that was just him. She couldn't fight him any longer. Emotions that had been building ever since Jennifer's arrest last year snapped and let go. Defeated, Maggie turned her head against his chest and let the tears come. Nate's shoulders relaxed and he tucked her against him, holding her while she finally let everything spill out.

Maggie knew it was wrong, but it felt right. Why now, after all this time, did she finally felt connected to someone? There were so many reasons why he was wrong for her. He was a man who lived for his work and thought nothing of putting himself in danger. He had his life ahead of him. They didn't even live in the same country.

And in a very short time, he'd be gone. And she was shocked to find, in the circle of his arms, that she would miss him.

But she had right now, and she burrowed deeper into his chest, letting the clean scent of him surround her. Letting his body form a cocoon as the slightest bit of healing trickled into her body.

The tears abated and she became aware of his hand running up and down her back, slowly and sure. She needed him on so many levels. Desire filled the raw, aching hole and she was tempted to channel everything into a physical manifestation. But that would be wrong.

His lips touched her ear and she turned towards them. He spoke instead.

"Trust me, Maggie," he whispered, and she shivered. "You need to talk to someone. And I'm here."

She wanted to trust him. It was part of the problem.

Maggie made herself pull away and look up into his face. *He's beautiful,* she thought, stunned. Not just his body, not just the colour of his eyes, the strong line of his lips or the cleft in his chin. But beautiful on the inside. Strong, yes, and stubborn. But principled and caring and compassionate. She wanted to share everything with him. Needed to. She'd pushed it down, pretended that the past didn't exist to everyone but herself. She couldn't do it anymore.

"What do you want to know?"

His lips curved ever so slightly. "Whatever you want to tell me. I want to know how Maggie Taylor ended up here. I want…"

He stopped and swallowed. Maggie's heart held a moment, waiting for what he'd say next. When he answered, it was as if he were touching her even though they were separated by inches.

"I want to know everything about you."

Maggie chafed her arms, already missing the warmth of his body. She was so tired. Tired of being governed by fear. She needed this.

"Then I'll tell you. Let's get a drink and start a fire. You might want to settle in for the duration."

He smiled. "One fire coming up."

Maggie got glasses and a bottle of rye whiskey from the cupboard. When she went into the living room, flames were licking warmly in the gas fireplace and Nate was sitting on the sofa, his elbows braced on his knees, staring into the orange blaze.

"Here. Hold these."

He held the glasses while she poured a small amount in the bottom of each one, then put the bottle down on the coffee table. She took a seat next to him, sipping the liquor. It warmed a path to her stomach, and she closed her eyes and sighed.

"Why don't you start at the beginning, Maggie. I know you lost your parents and your husband, but that really only scratches the surface." Nate's voice touched her, and she opened her eyes. He held her gaze so she couldn't back away. "There's clearly more. Like why it still hurts so much. How it's shaped you into who you are, how you got to be owner of a bed and breakfast in the middle of nowhere, looking after everyone else instead of yourself."

Maggie tucked her left foot under her leg, leaning back against the cushions. She had told herself that telling him, no matter how close they seemed to get, would be crossing a line. But they'd already crossed several lines with the kiss and with her sobbing all over him. Perhaps if he knew…really knew…who she was, it would actually have the opposite effect. Part of her wished it would be so. That perhaps the details would be sufficient to keep him at arms' length. What man wanted a woman still grieving for her loss and paralyzed by fear? It would be easier for her to resist him if he resisted her first.

And the other part of her yearned for him to listen, to understand, to accept.

"The beginning? Things were pretty normal for me growing up, until my parents died when I was a teenager and I had to look after myself." She took another fortifying sip of the rye. It sounded cut and dried now, but her whole world had been ripped apart, changing everything. She was no longer someone's daughter. She'd become Maggie, the orphan, trying to find her way.

"How did they die?"

"In a car accident."

His free hand dropped to her knee, stayed there. "I'm sorry. That must have been horrible for you."

"Thank you."

"Didn't you have anywhere to go?"

She smiled sadly. "Not really. And seeing I was the

age of majority, I looked after myself. Got a job. Tried to make some sense of things."

"And then?"

She looked down at the sight of his hand on her leg, wished fleetingly it didn't feel quite so good. She didn't feel like she was burdening him with prolonged grief. Nate didn't know her family, her friends. Knowing she could speak freely without the guilt she often felt when talking to others was a relief, and the words came easier with every breath.

She lifted her head and their eyes met. There was no pity on his face. She wouldn't have been able to take that. But there was compassion and patience, and she was grateful for it. The tension abated in her neck.

"Then I met Mike. He is my second cousin, the son of a cousin who had a baby far too young and made really bad choices, which resulted in Mike being put in foster care." She looked away from his hand and up into his eyes. "When I met him, I was twenty-two and he was eleven, still being bounced from home to home. And I suppose I thought, here is someone who is my flesh and blood, someone who knows what lonely means. It was the only hint of family I had and I needed to cling to it. Hadn't realized it until he was standing there in front of me."

"You needed him as much as he needed you."

Maggie nodded. She had. Mike had given her purpose. She doubted he knew to this day how much.

"I was working steadily, had an apartment in Sundre. I petitioned the court for guardianship and I got it. I don't know who was more surprised, me or Mike."

"You became each other's family."

"Yes, I suppose we did. Mike was a good kid, he was just scared. Didn't trust people much and I couldn't blame him. I did the best I could, but heck, I was young too and still raw from all I'd been through. I met Tom. Mike was a teenager when we got married and had Jen. I suppose he felt in the way after that, although he never said anything about it. Mike never talked about things like that much." She smiled at Nate. "Sounds like someone else I know. Anyway, by the time he graduated, he was rodeoing in season and working odd jobs in the off-times."

Her smile turned wistful. "I didn't think he'd ever find anyone to trust his heart to, but he did."

"Like you did with Tom?"

Maggie suddenly realized that she'd been talking, really talking, more than she'd planned. Maybe it was the fire, or the liquor, or the fact that Nate was safe and comfortable. Regardless, this afternoon they had turned a corner. Somewhere in the mess of confusion she'd made the decision to stop fighting and it shocked her to realize how quickly she'd dropped her guard.

But now Nate had turned the subject to Tom, and it was different than talking about Mike. She wasn't sure she could go on. Certainly not as easily as she'd talked about her cousin. Tom had done for her what Grace had done for Mike. Given her a place to put her heart for safekeeping. Or so she'd thought.

Losing him had been the most devastating thing she'd ever been through, and it had taken every ounce of her strength to put her life back together. Even now, pieces were missing, and it was incredibly painful. A memory flashed through her mind, not of Tom, but of Nate kissing her in the kitchen. The sheer beauty of it had scared her to death. It couldn't happen again. She couldn't feel like that again. The last time she'd had that depth of feeling, she'd ended up being crushed beneath it. It was an odd position to be in, trusting Nate yet needing to push him away.

Surely talking about one's dead husband would make any man put on the brakes.

"Yes. I did trust my heart to Tom."

"And then he died, and you were left with Jen."

Her throat closed up a bit and she nodded.

"Come here."

Nate took her glass away and deposited it on the table with his own. Shifting, he leaned back against the arm of the sofa, running one leg along the inside edge. She knew she should keep her distance, but he felt too good. Unresisting, she let him pull her back until she was cradled in the lee of his legs, his arms around her loosely, his fingers lightly circling her wrists.

"Oh, Nate." She sighed, staring into the dancing flames. Why did he have to be so perfect? Why was it that after all this time, Nate Griffith could make her feel things she hadn't felt in years? Including the need to spill about her past?

She paused for so long he squeezed her wrist. "You're thinking too much. Forget the reasons why and just let it out, Maggie. It's been in there a long time, hasn't it?"

She nodded.

He stroked her wrist bone with his thumb. "Can you tell me about him?"

Her throat thickened and she swallowed. "I don't know," she whispered, her voice thin in the rich air.

"I'd like to hear about it, if you want to tell me." He touched his forehead to her hair.

"You have to understand that I really don't talk about Tom. To anyone. Talking about him now... doesn't come easily."

Nate waited.

Maggie closed her eyes and absorbed the warmth and strength of his body into her soul. Why not tell him and be free of it? He'd be going back to his job in a few weeks and they'd never meet again. He'd forget all about her and her dead husband, after all. What would be the benefit of a quick fling? Because after the way he'd kissed her, she knew that was a distinct possibility. He'd leave her behind and she'd be left hurt, all over again. Because she didn't do casual, or temporary. And she didn't do serious relationships either.

He was alive, breathing, real. And if she weren't careful, she'd set herself up for hurt. It would be foolish to do that when it could easily be avoided. Maybe telling them would bring them closer in one way, but it should certainly cool the jets on any attraction between them.

"I was waitressing and Tom was working the patch." At Nate's pause, she amended, "The oil patch. He was doing security at a refinery north of town and used to come in for breakfast and pie in the mornings. The first time we met, I teased him about eating pie at six a.m."

An image flirted with her, Tom, young and energetic, blond and teasing dimples. She realized she'd been sitting for a few moments with a smile of remembrance on her lips. "Sorry."

"Don't be. Go on."

"I was trying to raise Mike, and working a couple of jobs to make ends meet. Tom was a breath of fresh air. For our first date, he packed a picnic and waited on me, since, he said, I was always waiting on him. I was twenty-three."

Colour crept into her cheeks. "I hadn't planned on life changing so quickly, but I fell hard and fast. I was starved for love and he was everything I could have imagined wanting. We got married three months later. Seven months after that Jen was born."

"And you moved here?"

She nodded. She remembered quite clearly the day he'd brought her here, late in the fall with Jen in a blanket in her arms. She'd been so angry with him when she'd found out he'd already bought it without consulting her. It was stupid, she realized later. Fighting over something so silly, when the truth was she'd adored the place as soon as she'd crossed the threshold. Drafty corners and all.

"Yes, we came here. He was making good money in the patch, and we could have the house and I could stay home and be with Jen. Maybe even have a few more."

Nate lifted his right hand from her arm, stroking her hair. "You wanted more children."

"I did then. He…" She stopped, unsure of how to go on. She did that a lot. She was unused to saying personal things aloud, but it seemed like it was all she'd been doing since Nate arrived. "He fixed something in me that had been broken when I lost my family."

"Only then he died, too."

"Yeah. And I think that day I realized that it didn't matter what I did, the people I loved were going to leave me. I only had Jen left."

"And that's why you worry about her so much. You're waiting for something to happen to her, too."

He understood.

Maggie felt all the panic and tension drain out of her body in one long, flowing river. The fact that it made sense to someone other than herself was liberating. "Yes."

Nate closed his eyes and cupped her head in his hand. All the resistance he'd felt vibrating through her body had melted away as she lay against his chest. Trusting, empty.

She'd been hurt so much. He really hadn't had any idea of how deep her hurt had gone. Maybe he should have, after today. The truth was he had wanted to know, to feel close to her. He cared about her, and he was shocked to realize it had only taken a few short days for his feelings to be involved.

But she'd given in easily, told him more than he'd ever expected, and he wasn't sure what to do with it.

The one thing he knew for sure, now more than ever, was that he couldn't be responsible for hurting her again. Maggie Taylor was too precious to be trifled with. He'd never met a woman with more pain, yet so strong. He couldn't imagine anyone picking up the pieces of their life in the way she had, with a baby and a foster child and a need to make a living. He knew for damned sure he couldn't be the one to turn that upside down.

Which made it insanely difficult, because he wanted her more than ever.

She'd trusted him today and he'd thought it was what he wanted. Now he knew that was a mistake. If she were to find out why he was really here, all that trust would be broken. No, it would have to be done clean. And when he left, it would be with a smile and warm memories of what they'd shared. How they'd helped each other. He felt the sting of irony that the truth would only tarnish the fleeting relationship they'd built.

It was how it had to be.

Long moments passed and he simply held her in his arms, felt her breathing, felt their connection growing and expanding. Never before had he felt so comfortable with a woman.

He looked around the room over the top of her head. Comfortable, welcoming, cozy. Like her. Yet…a blazing fire, a sparkling glass bottle of dark liquid, splashes of colour…vibrant. Also like her. A woman who made her living caring for others but one who knew how to stand on her own two feet. A survivor.

A woman he wanted. Completely.

But he couldn't have her. Not after all that had happened today. It would be completely unfair to her, in every way. He felt guilty enough about misleading her about his work. He knew for damn sure he wouldn't take advantage of her when she was stripped bare. Because he knew she hadn't told him every detail. He wondered how Tom had died. She hadn't told him about the troubles she'd had since, or Jen's brush with the law last year. And he wondered if she'd ever trust him enough to let him in completely.

So he held her in his arms as the afternoon wore on, wondering how the hell he was going to get through the next week.

8

Cooking. He watched her from the doorway, his arms folded over his chest as he leaned against the woodwork. He realized now it was what she did when she was particularly bothered or upset. After the events of the afternoon, he guessed they'd have a fine meal tonight.

She turned a beef mixture into a casserole as her brows pulled together in a frown. She lifted a fragile square of pastry and laid it over the top of the beef, pricking it with a fork. But he heard the deep sigh that seemed to come from her very toes.

"Penny for your thoughts."

She spun, her hand flying to her chest in surprise. He smiled. At least he could still surprise her.

"Only a penny?" She tried to joke, but her attempt at a jaunty grin wobbled. It appeared she hadn't bounced back as well as she was trying to portray.

"Maggie, are you sure you're okay?" He dropped his arms and started into the room.

She took a deep breath and squared her shoulders. "Of course I am."

She slid the dish into the oven. Turned and faced him, pasting on a smile that he understood was clearly for his benefit. She wiped her hands on her apron.

"It's chinooking. Which means tomorrow you'll be slogging it out in the muck."

He pushed away the urge to simply cross the floor and kiss her. He'd been thinking of it ever since she'd lain in his arms. But she was too raw, he could see that. "Chinooking?"

Maggie took a dishcloth and began wiping down the counter. "It's a wind that comes over the mountains, and it'll melt all the snow that's left. Some days it seems to blow and blow, but when it's done, it'll feel like spring around here."

Great. Warmer weather meant walking, and walking in muck. He'd actually hoped the cool weather would prevail a little longer. He frowned. Wished Maggie had an ATV he could borrow. Only then she'd ask why, and where he was going…dammit. Things were growing more complicated by the second.

"You don't have a headache, do you?" She took a few steps forward. "A lot of people get them, especially if they're not used to the pressure change. If your head is bothering you, I have acetaminophen in the cabinet."

She was the fragile one here and she was worried about his headache? The only headache he had wasn't from the pressure change, but from finding ways to keep his reasons for being here private without telling bald-faced lies. How to remain focused on his job without thinking about her every waking minute.

He was starting to fall for her, he realized. His head really did start to ache.

"My head is fine."

"Oh."

The short, quiet word told him he'd been too harsh, and he tried to soften his expression. He hadn't meant to snap at her. "But thanks for asking." He pushed his thoughts away and tried a smile. "How long until dinner?"

"About an hour."

Her reply was cool and he guessed she wasn't quite ready to forgive him for his snappishness. "I guess I'll go read or something, then."

"Nate?"

He paused. Lord, but she was beautiful. She'd wiped away any trace of her earlier tears and her eyes shone the most perfect shade of blue, like his grandmother's china bowl on his mom's cabinet, the one he was never allowed to touch as a boy. Blue Willow, he remembered now. Timeless and beautiful, like Maggie. Her lips were slightly puffed and he wanted to kiss them until they both ran out of breath. His chest tightened, strangling. He wanted to carry her upstairs, undress her, run his fingers over her creamy skin. Make love to her on the homemade quilt until the shadows grew long and disappeared. He wanted to tell her the truth and be free of it. He couldn't do any of those things.

She was watching him as though she could read his mind and he shuddered.

"What, Maggie." It came out almost a whisper and the line of tension crackled between them.

She broke eye contact first, and half turned, breaking the spell. "Let's go for a walk while dinner's cooking. I'll show you what a Chinook arch looks like."

Getting outside was probably a really, really good idea. Otherwise he'd do something foolish that he couldn't take back. Like kiss her again. Like tell her how he was feeling. Ridiculous.

They pulled on boots and jackets, leaving their hats behind and putting their hands in their pockets.

Once outside, Maggie led him down the drive to the road. It was paved, but barely. Narrow with no lines printed on it. Just a country road leading to the only place she'd called home in almost twenty years. He was a city boy, born and bred. The wide-open space, the simplicity of it, was a revelation. He breathed deeply, the sharp wind buffeting his chest. Felt a little of the tension slip away.

"See that?" She lifted her finger and pointed to the white sweep of clouds in the west. "That's a Chinook arch. Like a horizontal rainbow of cloud front. I've seen it warm over ten degrees Celsius in less than an hour. I've seen snow melt so quickly that you'd swear by the sound of the drips that it was raining."

"You love it here." He shook off the feeling of guilt from prying again, torn between caring for her and wanting to see the whole picture. It was like she was trying to forget all about their earlier conversation and pretend it had never happened.

She kept walking, and he listened as her footsteps

squeaked on the melting snow of the shoulder of the road.

"I've never been anywhere else. This is home."

"It's very different from where I'm from."

"Florida?"

He laughed. He'd only been in Florida for the last few years, although he loved it there and considered it his home base. "I was brought up in Philadelphia. Where my parents are. But yes, Florida too. Have you ever been?"

She shook her head. "I've been to Vancouver. Once."

They walked on, Maggie's hair blown back by the force of the westerly wind. "I always had Jen, and she had school. And during breaks, I always had guests. I've never had the chance to travel."

His chin flattened. "Until a few weeks ago, and you got saddled with me instead. I'm sorry about that."

He loved how she smiled back. It was free of agenda, unfettered by awkwardness and with a hint of growing trust at the corners. Had he inspired that?

"I'm starting to not regret that quite as much as I did at first." She tried tucking her hair behind her ears. "You've been everywhere, I suppose," she commented.

"I've been around. The Middle East, Europe with the Marines. All over North America with the Marshal Service. But…"

Maggie turned her head to look up at him, a strand of hair whipping around her face and catching in her mouth. She plucked it out with a finger. He reached out tucked it back, his finger lingering by her earlobe.

"But…"

He dropped his hand. He doubted she could really comprehend the places he'd been or the things he'd seen. "But there's no place like home. Other than my mom's place, here with you, at Mountain Haven, is as close as it gets."

"What about your place in Florida?" The moment suspended as the wind howled around them.

What about it? It was empty and functional and a place for him to sleep and eat. Had been for several months.

"My house there doesn't really feel like a home."

He could tell by the look in her eyes she wanted to ask more but didn't. Instead she placed a hand on his forearm, unaware of how the simple gesture touched him.

"Then I'm glad you're happy here."

That was it. He was surprised. Any woman he knew would have asked long ago if there was a wife or girl-friend in the wings. But not Maggie. He understood now that she'd learned long ago to simply accept. He almost wanted her to ask, just so he could tell her there was no one. No one with a claim on his heart.

Maggie turned to keep walking and he clasped her hand in his. She smiled softly, squeezing his fingers.

"Thank you, Nate, again. For being there today. It helped. More than you know."

Their hands swung gently between them as they ambled along rough pavement. It hit him as being a bit surreal, walking down a country road, holding hands with a beautiful woman. "Something's happening between us, Maggie, we both know it."

"I…I'm not prepared for that."

"I know."

His low words were almost lost in the power of the Chinook, but she heard them. He looked over at her, saw her swallow, look down at her feet as their steps slowed.

"Maggie, don't run, okay? We've both been dancing around it until neither of us knows how to act or what to say. So I'm just going to get it out of the way. I'm attracted to you. More than I thought possible."

Her mouth opened and shut a few times before she could speak. "I know. And I've started to trust you, Nate, and it scares me to death. I don't have it in me to start anything. There are so many reasons not to."

His lip curled at the thought of trust. The one bugbear in all of this was that he knew she trusted him more with each passing day. And he knew she shouldn't. Knew that she'd be more hurt if she knew he'd been keeping secrets all this time. He wondered again whether it would be better to just tell her.

Then he remembered the look in her eyes today when she'd thought Jen was hurt, when she'd told him about all the loss she'd suffered. He couldn't tell her and walk out the door each day that was left, knowing how she'd worry. She didn't need that. She had enough to worry about. Not only that, if he told her, he'd lose any hope of finding out what it was he already suspected. That Maggie knew a hell of a lot more than she was saying.

He felt her eyes on him and he turned his head, his face softening slightly. "Sorry. I didn't mean to disappear." He took her other hand in his, stopping their progress in the middle of the road, running his fingers over her soft knuckles.

He leaned forward, just a little, and touched his lips to her forehead, catching a strand of her hair in his mouth as the wind whipped it around. He pulled it out with a finger.

Their time together was growing short. He wouldn't have to worry about seeing her every day, knowing he was keeping secrets from her. Another week was all that was left in his stay and they would probably never see each other again.

It was crazy how empty the thought of that made him feel.

Her hair whipped around and he reached out, threading his fingers through the long strands, pushing them back so her pale face was framed by the darker skin of his hands. It was wrong to feel this way and he knew it. But in the end the pull to her was too strong to fight.

"I'm sorry, Maggie. I have to."

He pulled gently with his hands, drawing her closer and up, dipping his head until he touched her lips with his.

She was sweet, so very sweet, and a little salty from her earlier tears. His eyes slammed shut and he focused on the feel of her, real and alive and responsive. Despite her earlier protests, despite all the reasons why she couldn't, her mouth opened beneath his and he squared his feet, planting his weight, taking it as deep and as dark as she'd let him.

The wind howled around them, warm and wild, swirling up dust. He lowered one hand, pressing it to the small of her back, pulling her closer so that their bodies were meshed as closely as their outerwear would allow. Her arms reached up, circled his neck as she adjusted the angle of her head to better fit his and his blood sang. He gripped her hair, tugging to tilt her head back and he ripped his mouth from hers, sliding his tongue up her neck.

She whimpered, and he felt the vibration on his lips.

He froze. God, here he was doing the very thing he'd promised himself he wouldn't, not today. This was what going for a walk had been meant to avoid. Breathing heavily, he gently released her and backed away.

"You're stopping." Her cheeks flamed, but she met his eyes bravely.

"You're too vulnerable, Maggie. We both know it."

"I think I'm old enough to know what I want." She lifted her chin.

He couldn't stop the surge at her words. She wanted him. That was clear. Her response had told him plainly she wanted him as much as he wanted her.

Maggie held his gaze, trying to seem stronger than he knew she felt. She wasn't the kind to take something to a physical level and be cavalier about it. He took a step backwards. "But I'm not sure you'd see it the same way tomorrow, and I don't want to take advantage. And the last thing I want to do is hurt you in any way." He tried slow, steadying breaths. "Besides, were in the middle of the road."

Maggie looked left and right while the only sound was the Chinook and dripping water from melting snow. Then she snorted, a tiny, ladylike bubble.

"Oh goodness, we are, aren't we?"

"Yeah."

Things seemed back to normal for a few minutes. They turned back in the direction they'd come, and the wind was at their backs, buffeting them along. Maggie tried tucking her hair behind her ears, but it wouldn't stay. It blew wildly about her head.

It was good they'd stopped when they had.

When the reached the lane up to the house, she stopped suddenly. He looked at her, then at the house. It seemed to be waiting for them to go in.

"So what do we do now?"

Nate knew what he wanted to do, but it would cause more problems that it would solve. He sighed.

"Damned if I know, Maggie. Damned if I know."

———

Maggie hummed as she folded the clothes in her basket, placing them in two piles on her bed; one for her, one for Nate. He'd offered to do his own laundry if she'd let him use her facilities, but she didn't mind doing it for him. When she'd offered, there'd been a slightly tense moment as she'd worried he'd think she was just after billing the service.

Truth be told, it was nice to have someone to do for.

Washing his clothing was nothing at all. She'd merely made the comment that she could throw it in with her own and the awkward moment had passed.

She smoothed her hand over a pair of his jeans, rubbing out the creases from the dryer. Her fingers lingered over the denim, picturing how the fabric molded to his frame. Not in many, many years had she felt such a need for a man, such desire. Not only that, but she'd never expected that she'd find those things that made him a cop—the haircut, the penchant for neatness, the physicality—so alluring.

When he was gone on his ramblings during the day, she couldn't believe how wantonly she'd behaved during their walk. In the middle of the road, of all things. But the moment his arms went around her and he kissed her, she forgot everything beyond the feel and taste of him. For those few moments, she forgot the fear. When she was in his embrace, she forgot all the reasons why he was wrong for her. He made her feel young and alive and the novelty was intoxicating.

They'd walked back to the house and she'd wondered how on earth they were going to coexist in the same house for the next several days. Wanting him to kiss her again, knowing it was inadvisable. Wanting much more from him, yet afraid to take that giant step into being intimate with a man. She didn't take those things lightly.

But she needn't have worried at all. Nate had reverted to his pleasant, normal self. Full stop. No more long looks, intimate smiles, toe-curling kisses. None.

And she missed him.

The laundry finished, she put her own clothes away and stacked his, along with the guest towels, back in the basket to take upstairs to his room. Maybe he'd put on the brakes because she'd never given him a reason to move forward. And yes, he was only here for a short time. But he understood her. That much she knew. She'd trusted him with her past and that was a subject she rarely talked about. And he'd made the first move each time they'd kissed, touched.

What if he was waiting for her to make a move now?

Maggie swallowed as saliva pooled in her mouth. After seventeen years of celibacy, she was afraid. Afraid of looking silly. Afraid of the intensity. Afraid of another man seeing her body. She wasn't twenty anymore. She'd had a child. She'd aged. And his body was youthful and perfect.

"Maggie?"

Nate called as he came in the door and she couldn't stop the flood of welcome that rushed through her. When had she started truly looking forward to his return every day?

"I'm in here."

She let out a slow breath. This was silly. He was only a man. This was only a crazy reaction to having him so close; to being alone together.

She hefted the laundry basket, setting it on her hip. It wasn't in her to make the next move. No matter how much she wanted to.

She turned the corner into the kitchen, the basket sliding off her hip to the floor as she saw his face.

"Have you got bandages, Maggie?"

His voice was calm, reasonable, but all Maggie saw was blood streaming from a gash that ran down his forehead to just below his eyebrow.

"Maggie. Bandages."

She sprang into action, the sight of the cut always before her eyes as she ran to the bathroom for the first-aid kit.

When she came back, he'd pulled out a kitchen chair and sat in it. Maggie grabbed an ivory hand towel from the spilled basket and immediately pressed it to the cut, staunching the blood as it seeped darkly through the cotton. "Hold this for a minute."

She opened the kit and saw her fingers trembling. He was fine, it was just a cut, she reassured herself. But seeing the blood, the open gash, had sent pins and needles through her extremities. What if he had a concussion, or needed stitches?

She looked up, gauze and scissors in her hand, and watched as Nate's face paled and he weaved slightly.

She dropped the items to the floor and knelt before him, pressing one hand to the towel and the other to the back of his head, pushing him forward.

"Put your head between your knees," she commanded, hoping to God he didn't pass out or get sick. Either one might mean concussion.

He obeyed, saying nothing.

"Take slow, deep breaths, Nate."

She moved to the side a bit, still holding the towel to the wound and rubbing a hand over his shoulders. The movement gave her time to find her own bearings, and she realized something shocking.

In the instant she'd seen his blood, known he was injured, her only thoughts had been for him. Not of Tom. Not of Jen. Not of fear borne from years of loss and anxiety. But for *him*.

It was more than lust, more than feeding a hunger. It was Nate, the man, and he inspired feelings Maggie had thought long extinct. For her, it had suddenly become much deeper and meaningful. And complicated.

"I'm okay now."

His voice came through, deep and rough and she blinked back tears at the mere sound of it.

"Sit up slowly, that's it." She helped guide him up until he was upright in the chair once more. Once he was stable, she put his hand on the towel and moved quickly to grab a chair so she could sit facing him.

"I'm going to pull the towel away now," she murmured, gently pulling the cotton from his head. She swallowed at the amount of blood staining the ivory. With light fingers, she held his forehead and examined the cut. "You should have stitches."

"I'll be fine, just bandage it up."

"Nate, it's huge. Even with stitches, you'll likely have a scar. You can guarantee it if I patch you up. Not to mention it'll take longer for it to heal."

"There's steri-tape in my bag. I'll get it."

"Tell me where it is and I'll get it for you."

"No. I mean, I'm feeling much better."

"Don't be stupid. You asked for my help, let me give it."

"The bleeding's nearly stopped. I'll get the tape and let you do it, alright?"

She sat back at his sharp tone. She wasn't sure why she'd been so worried if he were going to be this stubborn. Men. Why was it that admitting they needed help was so difficult?

He got up from his chair and made his way to the stairs.

She took the towel and threw it in the trash; there was no saving it. What on earth had happened to him, and how long had he walked before getting to the house?

"Maggie."

Her head snapped up. Nate's voice was weak and thready. She rushed towards the stairs. Why hadn't he let her go after the supplies rather than playing the tough guy?

"Oh my stars, Nate."

He was half-way down the stairs, clinging to the banister and holding a small kit in his hands.

She went up half a dozen steps and slid beneath his right arm, bolstering his weight. "You big ninny. Trying to do this yourself. From now on, you're doing exactly what I tell you."

"Yes ma'am."

Carefully they made their way to the bottom of the stairs and she helped him back to the chair. He sat heavily, closed his eyes while she took the kit from his hands.

"This isn't my forte, just so you know. You really should see a doctor."

"No doctors. It's just a scratch."

"Don't be stupid."

A muscle in his jaw ticked. "I just don't like doctors,

okay? I've had worse wounds, trust me. I've been patched up by medics, by colleagues and even by a tribal leader in Africa."

"You are so stubborn." Maggie held the first strip of tape. "Take a breath. Now let it out. Slowly."

As he exhaled, she pushed the edges of the wound together and applied the tape.

His eyes opened, the blue-green of the sun through a bottle. They focused on her face. "Thank you for doing this."

She caught the tip of her tongue in her teeth as she applied the next strip.

"I want it noted that I thought you should see a professional."

His gaze never wavered, and her stomach tumbled, both from the first aid and from his intense focus.

"You can charge for services rendered. I'll speak up for you."

Her lips twitched. "You're not that badly injured, if you're cracking jokes."

"It's a scratch," he repeated. "I've got scars much worse."

Her hand halted, another strip of tape stuck to her index finger. She wondered where he had scars; what they looked like. Her body heated as she imagined touching him, kissing all the places where they marked his skin.

And just as quickly, she cooled. She couldn't forget that the very presence of the scars were a real reminder of the life he led. And the danger he represented.

"What happened, anyway?"

He cleared his throat. "I was walking the creek. Don't know exactly what happened, but I must have slipped in some mud. Hit my head on a rock, I guess. And got my bell rung pretty good."

Maggie reached for a swab, cleaned the bottom of the cut and reached for the gauze. It made sense, she supposed. The creek bank could be slick this time of year, and a stripe of dried mud ran up his leg.

"And you walked all the way back here with your head bleeding."

He nodded slightly, wincing. "Yeah. Used a mitten to control the bleeding—it's a write off by the way—and hit for home."

She sat back, packing the kit again. "You're patched up, for what it's worth. I still think you're probably concussed."

"Then you'll have to keep an eye on me, won't you?"

He smiled his most charming smile, and suddenly the life went out of her legs.

She sat heavily. She hated the sight of blood, but her immediate concern for his health had overridden it. Now that he was attended to, the aversion came back heavy and strong. The smell of blood was the smell of death. She would have taken him to the hospital out of sheer worry, but she didn't like hospitals any more than he apparently did. Hospitals were always a reminder of what she'd lost.

"You need tea, Maggie. Now you're pale."

She nodded. "I'll make some. I think we could both use it. I've got to keep my eye on you for the next while."

She would have moved to get up but he stayed her

with a hand on her knee. "I don't know how to thank you. You've always gone above and beyond, but today… that's different. I owe you, Maggie."

She rose, his hand sliding off her leg. "It's fine. It's the smell of the blood, that's all."

She forced herself to smile. He couldn't know, and she didn't want him to. For all he was aware, Tom had been killed on the job. And he had been. But it hadn't been an accident. No indeed. Tom had been shot. And by the time she'd reached the hospital he was in a coma. He'd never regained consciousness. All she had for parting memories were the sights and smells of his blood.

Too late she realized she was trembling. Nate lifted his hand and cupped her jaws with his fingers, steadying her. It was the most natural thing in the world to put her arms around him, try to gain strength from his.

He pulled her close and she linked her hands behind his back.

That's when she felt it beneath her fingers, hard and cold.

She pushed out of his arms.

"You're carrying a gun."

9

Maggie stepped back, away from him. She could still feel the cold lump of the steel, the shape of it, tucked into the waistband of his jeans.

He was in her house, carrying a weapon. He had to have brought it with him, she realized. He'd had it all along. Her blood ran cold at the thought. In those moments all of Maggie's old feelings reared up, making her next words strangled and raw.

"You're carrying a gun."

The words echoed through the room. For long seconds Nate simply stared at her, as if determining what would be the best thing to say. She drew in a shaky breath. Tom had carried a handgun during his duties. To her recollection, he'd never fired it.

Not until the night he'd had to protect himself. Not until the night he'd come face to face with another weapon and he'd fired back. The end result was that he'd lived long enough to make it to hospital and the other man hadn't. And because the trespasser—a so-

called activist—had also died, it didn't matter that Tom
had died defending himself. His name had been sullied
by the press, bandied about in the news like some polit-
ical trick. One side placing the blame on him, the other
side blaming the other man. Maggie had been caught
in the middle, trying to grieve and defend him while
being left alone with an infant daughter and a teenage
cousin.

The very thought of Nate carrying a gun and being
so calm about it made her sick to her stomach. She'd
trusted him. He'd told her about his leave of absence,
and she'd believed him. Now she realized it was all a lie.
The day it had hit her—he was on assignment—she'd
known. And she'd let him divert her from the truth. But
a man on a leave of absence, on vacation, didn't carry
a gun.

Maggie folded her hands, keeping them from
fidgeting and twisting by sheer willpower. He'd more
than misrepresented himself to her. He'd insinuated a
place for himself at Mountain Haven. *With* her.

She swallowed against the bile in her throat. He'd
known all along and yet he'd let things grow between
them. The sting of betrayal was made worse by her
acute embarrassment at her own actions. She'd kissed
him. Wanted him. She'd started to care for him, deeply.
Had considered taking it further, knowing he was leaving. Thank goodness she hadn't articulated her feelings.
She clenched her fingers, turning the tips white. But she
refused to turn away. Gathering all her strength, she
squared her chin.

"Get out."

Nate froze. "You want me to leave?" He picked his words carefully, keeping his voice neutral.

"Do you or do you not have a gun tucked into the back of your jeans?"

She already knew the answer even as he sighed. At his brief silence, she raised an eyebrow.

"Yes, Maggie. I'm carrying a weapon."

She folded her arms, putting even more distance between them. "Why would that be, Nate? Am I some kind of threat to you?"

"I'm a marshal, Maggie. I don't go anywhere without a weapon. Ever."

Instead of reassuring her, her lips thinned. She'd accepted him at face value, and it had been a terrible mistake on her part. She'd believed everything he'd said, had wanted to help him. Had wanted to nurture him. Knowing she'd been duped stung her pride, her self-judgment. She asked the question simply to clarify what she already knew.

"You mean you've had a gun on you the whole time you were here?"

"Yes, Maggie."

She swallowed. She had to know all of it. Know how blind she'd been to what was going on around her. There was no turning back now. "When we went to Olds?"

"Yes." His eyes settled on hers steadily. She wanted him to look guilty, but he didn't. She wrinkled her brow. If she didn't know better, she'd almost think he looked relieved.

"When you went snowshoeing?"

"Yes."

"And walking each day?"

She wished he'd show some emotion, rather than standing tall, unflinching before her. His eyes were honest but unreadable, a look she realized he probably used in his job every day.

"Yes."

Maggie paused; her eyes widened. "The day we went walking in the Chinook?"

She waited for his answer, her heart in her throat. That day she'd been vulnerable, and that day she'd made the choice to trust him with much of herself. He'd held her as she'd cried in his arms, listened as she'd told him about Tom. She couldn't have been so wrong, could she?

"Yeah. That day too." His eyes searched hers, like he was asking her to understand. But she didn't understand anything. He hadn't really told her anything. How could he have held her and kissed her and been kind all the while having a handgun tucked in his jeans?

She turned away and he bent a little, trying to explain.

"Maggie, listen, what I said is true. I don't go *anywhere* without a gun." He stepped forward, holding out a hand, but she backed away. If he was asking her to say it was all right, to understand why he'd done it, he could forget it. She'd been honest with him. He obviously didn't think he needed to reciprocate.

"It's a part of who I am," he continued. "You shouldn't take it personally."

"Not take it personally?" Maggie raised her voice,

and she laughed a little at the end, the sound sharp and dry with disbelief. How could he possibly think she wouldn't take it personally? He'd come into her home. He'd brought guns into her home. And he hadn't told her. What else hadn't he told her? Was his whole story a fabrication?

She pointed to the door. "I want you to leave, Nate. You can get in your truck and drive into Olds and find a room at a motel. I'm sure your superiors will pay for it."

"I can't do that."

His reply was strong and definite, like he was giving an order, she thought. It would be much easier if he'd look away, or at least have the grace to look uncomfortable. But he kept her pinned with his eyes, begging her to understand. To accept. She'd done enough accepting. She'd accepted the death of her parents, leaving her orphaned. She'd accepted Tom's death, accepted the findings of the RCMP in their official report. She'd accepted Jen's troubles and had taken them on herself, done what she could to minimize the damage. She'd let Nate into her house and accepted his story about the girl as his reason for being here.

But she was done. She refused to turn away from him. He had to know she meant what she said. She leveled her gaze. "You're not welcome here. Not with your weapons."

"Maggie, you have to listen to me." He implored her with an outstretched hand, but she took another step backward. "I have to be here. *I have to.*"

"Why? Why here? And tell me the truth. I think I've earned it."

"Because I've been put here. I wish I could tell you more. But I can't. It's for your own protection."

She half turned, refusing his reply. It wasn't enough. Her heart pounded. All the little feelings she'd had but dismissed over the past few weeks bubbled up again. Tiny things that hadn't added up but that now made sense. "You're not on leave, are you?"

"No, I'm not."

Those three words took the starch out of her knees. She reached out and gripped the back of a chair. *His* chair, the one he sat at during meals and with his morning coffee.

She looked away, staring past him towards the kitchen window. Outside she could see her grass, working hard to grow and turn green, and the dark earth of the garden, yet to be planted. This was her world. The one that had been her mainstay for years. Her safe place. Right now, she wished she could get it back, that sense of normalcy. Wished she could forget all the long-forgotten things Nate had made her feel. That extraordinary world, with him, wasn't real. Knowing he'd deceived her made her long to return to normal more than anything.

At her long silence, he added quietly, "If it's worth anything, I didn't like it. Didn't like having to pretend."

"It's not worth much. It was all a lie then," she affirmed. She walked over to the counter and braced her hands on the top. The first time she'd considered truly moving on, doing something adventurous, out of her normal pattern, and this is what came of it. She'd felt safe with him. How could her judgment have been so off? She felt like a complete fool.

"Not all of it." He finally moved, going to stand behind her, yet keeping a subtle distance. He was close enough she could just feel the warmth of his breath on her neck. It made her remember how he tasted, how his arms felt, strong and sure around her. She had to stop thinking about it. It had been nothing more than momentary weakness. A flaw she wouldn't repeat.

"I was put on leave. The story I told you was one hundred percent true. But I was called back to work before it was over."

"And you're here on assignment." Everything she thought she knew melted away, leaving a dry, empty hole.

"I'm sorry, Maggie."

Nate wanted to go to her, pull her into his arms and beg her to understand, but he wouldn't do that to her. He'd already done enough. He could see that as she spun to face him, her eyes wide with shock at the turn of the afternoon. He shoved his hands into his pockets to keep from reaching out. This was exactly what he hadn't wanted to happen. But his earlier encounter changed everything.

"What sort of assignment brings you to the middle of nowhere, Alberta? I don't understand. How do you even have jurisdiction here?"

He wished he could tell her everything, but he couldn't, not yet. Not without clearing it first. "I can't tell you the specifics."

She snorted. "Of course not. I'm just supposed to

accept what you've told me and be a good girl and not question, right? I'm sorry, I can't do that."

Nate's frustration bubbled over. "Don't you think I wanted to tell you? Every time I looked into your eyes? Every time I kissed you, or you told me a little more about yourself? I hated having to lie to you, Maggie! But there's bigger issues at stake here!"

The outburst cost him. His head pained sharply and he exhaled slowly, trying to will it away. Shouting at her wouldn't solve anything.

"How on earth could I know that?" Her shout echoed through the kitchen.

This was why he'd kept the plan from her. Knowing what he knew about Peter Harding had made it clearer than ever that he had to keep her from harm. The more people knew, the more danger they would all be in. If Peter found out who he was and where he was staying, they could lose their opportunity. Or worse. No, it was necessary they keep it on a need-to-know basis. He reminded himself of that, drawing on all his strength to try to make her see reason.

"I know. And that's part of why I didn't say anything. You'd naturally have questions. Worries. I wanted to tell you, I did. I have reasons why I didn't."

"I don't care about your reasons." She tried to slide past him, but he caught her with a hand on her wrist.

"Maggie, don't. Let me give you what I can. Sit down and we'll talk."

Nate kept the pressure on her wrist. He looked down at his fingers circling the pale skin of her arm. Why did he care? His cover was blown. Maggie knew who he was. How long before she put the rest together? But that wasn't all. He'd known all along he wasn't being honest and he'd gotten close to her anyway. And more than trying to find out information. He'd started to get involved with her personally. He couldn't begin to count the mistakes he'd made.

He should let her walk away and get on with the job, get it finished and get out. But he couldn't. Couldn't let her think everything between them had been a lie. Because it hadn't been. It had been, perhaps, the most real thing he'd experienced in a long time.

He cared about her. And not just the physical attraction, although there was that. He cared about Maggie, her hurts, her fears. Wanted to protect her. Wanted… damn. He wanted to love her, if it came to that.

"It wasn't all a lie," he began. But stopped, looking away for a moment. What was he trying to do? Get her to butt out or make her understand how deep his feelings really went? Trying to argue semantics wasn't the right strategy.

Maggie was glaring at him like he was the villain, for God's sake. The horrible thing was, he felt like a villain. All because he hadn't been able to be honest with her all along. And because he still couldn't. Not about the case, not about his feelings for her. Grant had been specific in keeping Maggie out of the loop until they knew for sure; to protest he cared about her would only come across as a diversion.

"Don't try to justify it now, just because you're caught."

"I won't."

She'd asked earlier if she were a threat, and she'd been sarcastic. But the answer that had jumped into his brain at the time had been *more than you know*. It was true in more ways than one. In the back of his mind, he remembered what Grant had told him that day at the coffee shop. His gut said he could trust her. But what if he was wrong? After what had happened before his leave, he wasn't sure he trusted his instincts anymore. What if Grant's suspicions were true and Nate let personal feelings get in the way? It would ruin everything. There was no way he could put people in danger based on a feeling. It was too much of a risk.

Right now he had to decide exactly how much to tell her. Enough to ease her mind and not enough to compromise things. Smooth things over. Get her to let him stay long enough to finish the job. He couldn't let his growing feelings for her cloud the priority. He pushed away the need to pull her into his arms, kiss away the hurt marking her face right now. He wasn't foolish enough to think she was only angry at him. She was hurt too, and she had every right to be. What a mess.

He released her wrist and forced himself to relax, once muscle at a time, to make his body and expression as normal as possible. As he did it, her response mirrored his, until they both were more at ease.

"I'm asking you, please. Give me a chance to explain."

She hesitated long enough he took the opportunity to press his case. "I owe you an explanation. Let me give it."

She nodded and led the way back to the kitchen table. His head was aching now that the adrenaline had burned off, but he forced it to the back of his mind. He could take something for the pain later.

He sat heavily, turning the chair to the side so he was facing her. "You know that Grant and I met at a conference in Toronto a few years ago. When this case came up, it was a natural fit for me to work with him on it. It was all set up before I had a chance to think."

"So you're working with Grant." She crossed her right leg over her left.

"He's the local liaison, yes. And it's true, I was on a leave of absence and they brought me back. At the time it seemed the logical cover. It's a small town, Maggie. What would people say if they knew I was here? I had to keep under the radar. It was much easier to come under the ruse of a vacation. Only…only I met you and I hated lying to you from the beginning."

"He says conveniently."

She was going to be a hard sell, especially without the details she seemed so intent on getting. Right now she was sitting in her chair, legs crossed and arms folded close to her body. Defensive to cover the pain. Unwilling to listen. Her eyes evaded his as he attempted to make contact. She had every reason to be hurt. He'd let himself become personally involved with her under false pretenses. He knew better.

"I still don't understand how someone from the States gets to come up here. Isn't there a whole jurisdiction issue?"

This was the one part Nate knew he could explain

easily. "There's a Memorandum of Understanding between the US authorities and Canadian. I liaise with a local department or contact, and here I am."

"So when you met Grant, it wasn't about catching up."

"No. We were information sharing."

"And you'd deliberately come along that day. When I took Jen to the bus station." Her arms crossed tighter. Her blue eyes flashed, accusing. She deserved an honest answer. He wished he could give her one, prevent her from building a wall around herself. He didn't want her to shut him out. Even if what Grant thought was true, the more he could keep Maggie out of it now, the better. He could at least give her some kind of protection.

"I did. We met to discuss…details."

"Who could you possibly be looking for?"

Nate sat back in the chair. This was the one question he couldn't answer right now. How could he tell her? She was more wrapped up in it than she knew. It wasn't only the proximity that made her the perfect choice. And how on earth could he ask her what he needed to know? Grant had aired his suspicions and Nate admitted to himself that they weren't groundless. The problem was, he'd lost his objectivity. The evidence on paper didn't fit the person sitting before him now. There was more at stake than just the two of them. He had to be cautious.

"I can't tell you that."

"Again, convenient." She pushed her chair back but he put both hands on her thighs, keeping her seated.

"It's for your protection, Maggie, can't you see that?"

"Frankly, I can't."

The pounding in his head was increasing. It didn't matter that he'd been hit today. They had to move and move now. If he ruined this case, there'd be no leave of absence. Two mistakes in a row wouldn't go over well. But it was more than that. Maggie was at the centre of it, whether she knew it or not. Things would escalate from this moment forward. He had to take the time to explain things best he could. For now. Then he'd deal with her innocence. He knew in his heart that whatever Maggie had done, it had been unwittingly. Had to have been.

They should have had more time to make their move against Harding. But Nate had been distracted, he'd gotten careless. He'd ventured in closer to the farm and was on his way back out again when Pete had driven up in his truck. Nate had stopped, intending to see what was in the back of the vehicle when he'd frightened a flock of geese. The resulting flapping of wings and honking had sent up the alarm and he saw the rifle. And it hadn't been pointed at the birds.

He'd made himself a moving target, but Pete was a good shot. A graze was lucky.

He couldn't blame her for being scared. And she was under the impression that he'd only taken a fall.

The silence drew out as they stared at each other.

It was like they were holding a conversation without saying any words. When she finally spoke, he understood exactly what she was asking.

"When?"

Nate stood, walked a few feet and hooked his thumbs in his belt loops. Maggie looked away. He understood why. And hated it. It would be unfair of him to ask her for more.

"Tomorrow morning, best guess."

"So soon." The words were strangled.

"We need to move fast, before he takes off again."

"Who he?"

The name sat on his tongue and he debated. What would she do if he told her? And had Harding found out where he was staying yet?

Lord, he'd gotten careless and had put her in danger anyway. They had to strike first before Harding had a chance to regroup. He looked into Maggie's ashen face. And ignored the evidence for once. She was as innocent in all this as Jen had been. He'd stake his life on it. "I promise I'll tell you. Tonight."

"Nate, you'll be in danger," she repeated.

"I know." He ignored the searing pain in his head and squared his shoulders. "But this is what I'm trained for, Maggie. It's what I do, and I do it well."

"And afterwards?"

She had to know how this was all going to end. There could be no other way. "Afterwards Grant and I transport him back to the U.S. to stand trial."

This would be his last night at Mountain Haven. They both knew it. What Nate wanted and what he knew was possible were two very different things. He wanted to be with her. To love her. To take away that beautiful memory. Instead, he'd be planning an op. Working to keep her safe. The thought left him hollow.

"This person is wanted. A *fugitive*, Maggie. It's what I do. I bring in criminals who are running from the law. Do you think we go after the small-time shoplifters? Do you?"

To his relief she stayed put in her chair. Her face paled further, and her eyes widened. He hadn't wanted to frighten her but perhaps now it was the only way. To make her see why he'd felt the need for keeping her in the dark.

"The people I bring in are armed robbers, murderers, rapists, child predators. What do you think could happen if someone like that knew I was here to find them, knew you were involved?"

"If you're trying to scare me, it's working."

"Good. Because that's how important this is. It's the reason—the *only* reason—I had to keep quiet."

She looked away. "It doesn't change that you…"

He swallowed. She was right. He'd put his feelings for her above his duty. It was the first time he'd ever done that and he knew it had been a mistake. It served no purpose save to hurt both of them.

"No, it doesn't. I let myself become personally involved with you and I had no right. If you'd been anyone else…"

"You'd what?"

His breath caught as she turned liquid blue eyes on him. It was a day of truths. All too soon he'd be gone and perhaps if she knew, she'd accept his partial silence a little easier.

"I'd never have started to fall for you."

Calmly she rose from her chair. "You deceived me, used me. There is no excuse for that. You blew it, Nate."

I sure did, he thought, watching her walk away.

"Maggie."

She stopped at the doorway, refusing to turn around and face him.

"Can I stay, Maggie?"

Her words came, brittle. "I honour my commitments. I accepted your reservation, and your bill is paid."

On the contrary, he knew he'd be paying for this for a long time to come. A day wouldn't go by that he wouldn't think of her. The scent of vanilla and cinnamon, the sound of her laugh or howl of the westerly wind.

Maggie disappeared into her living quarters and Nate sighed. There was a lot to be done and a limited amount of time. He'd have to sort things out with her later. Right now he had a phone call to make.

They couldn't let Pete slip through their fingers again. He had to call Grant, assemble the team and prepare to go in. And add attempted murder to the list of charges.

Because he knew he'd gotten lucky. And he couldn't count on his luck to hold.

———

MAGGIE HELD IT ALL IN UNTIL SHE WAS IN HER LIVING quarters. She shut the door with a firm click, then went and sat in the chair by the window, staring outside but seeing nothing.

Had he really fallen for her? Or was that his way of trying to smooth things over?

She didn't know what to believe anymore. She only knew that for the first time since Tom's death, after all those long, lonely years, she'd finally let someone in. She'd finally started to care. It had gone beyond simple flirtation and the physical. She'd *fallen*. She'd fallen for the man she thought he was. Kind, caring, strong, trustworthy.

Now she felt like a complete fool.

In the isolation of her room, she let the tears come. Tears for all she'd lost, tears of humiliation. She hated her weakness, for allowing herself to fancy he was truly interested in her. She'd spent the majority of her life seeing things exactly as they were.

And where they were right now was that she was a forty-two-year-old widow with a teenage daughter and a bed and breakfast. Full stop. After years of protecting her heart, she'd let down her guard and had become vulnerable, trusting. She'd cautioned herself not to let herself get hurt again but she'd done it anyway. She'd let herself be seduced by the magic and romance of the situation, conveniently forgetting that reality would come crashing through.

She'd been stupid to believe he'd wanted her. She'd been naïve. He was staying now, but not for her. For the job.

She should have done *her* job and put a stop to any personal connections they'd made. She'd been foolish and fanciful and…weak. The tears were bitter and cold, and she resented them nearly as much as she resented Nate right now. Damn him for making her feel this way…hopeless and vulnerable. She hadn't cried often since Tom's death, and not once had it been over a man. Until now.

She swiped her hands roughly over her cheeks, brushing away the moisture. She'd indulged enough. She went to the bathroom and washed her face, covered the redness with makeup, and vowed she'd never cry over a man ever again.

He was gone from the kitchen when she entered it again. The remnants of her first-aid treatment had disappeared too, except for a bottle of acetaminophen that remained on the counter beside an empty glass. She should have realized his head would be hurting after the bump he'd taken.

The house was deathly silent. If he were concussed, he shouldn't be sleeping. Or if he did, she should at least wake him frequently. Just because she was angry and hurt didn't mean she wanted anything to happen to him.

She went upstairs, her feet creaking on the old steps, sounding louder than normal in the awkward silence that seemed to envelop the house. She should have insisted he see a doctor.

His door was open a crack and she tapped gently, pushing it open a few inches.

"Come in, Maggie."

Her body trembled at the sound of his soft, sure voice. In her anger it had been easy to believe he'd felt nothing for her, had used her. But as she pushed the door open with a squeak, and faced his eyes as they looked at her, she knew there was something between them. Something tenuous and tender, and now tainted with mistruths.

He was different, even if it was only her own perception that made him so. He wasn't Nate Griffith, reevaluating, but Nate Griffith, U.S. Marshal, back on the job.

"You're awake. I was worried."

He was sitting in the straight-backed chair, and the laptop was open in front of him. He spun so that he was facing the door, but he didn't get up. As much as she hated the lies, as much as she hated the guns…something about him made her feel safe. It had always been that way; hating what he did while still feeling proud and protected.

His flak jacket lay on the bed in plain sight. There was no point in hiding it from her now. She could say she didn't care about him all she wanted. The surge of relief she felt knowing he'd at least had a vest on told the truth.

"I didn't mean to worry you. Believe me, Maggie. I wanted to save you more worry. You've had your fair share."

"I saw the pills downstairs. Does it hurt much?"

Automatically his fingers found the bandage on his forehead and he winced. She fought back the urge to go to him and examine the wound.

"It's paining a bit yet. Nothing I can't handle."

"You shouldn't sleep for long periods of time. I'm pretty sure you probably have a concussion." Her fingers curled on the doorknob. Her first instinct was to care for

him. But things were too tenuous between them. She
didn't want him to think all was forgiven just because
she was concerned about his medical well-being.

"Me too. That's why I'm…" He paused, then
unsmiling, treated her with the truth. "That's why I'm
working."

Her muscles stiffened. "Working."

He nodded. "The investigation is moving forward
quickly now. We need to speak about that."

Her head spun as all the possibilities ricocheted in
her mind. She couldn't imagine an empty house again,
without him to cook for, talk to, laugh with. How could
that be, knowing what she knew now?

He'd be going away. But before that, she supposed
he'd get what he'd come for. And that wasn't her, even as
a tiny voice inside her wanted it to be. And after what
he'd said…there would be risks.

She kept her hand on the knob of the door. Better
she know now. Other than Jen and Mike, it had seemed
like everyone she'd cared about in her life had met a
tragic ending. And even Jen could have been in more
trouble if Maggie hadn't worked hard to change things.
It would be better all around if she kept her distance
from Nate.

"What do I have to do with it?"

He glanced at the laptop and her eyes followed. It
seemed to be some sort of mapping diagram. She knew
without him saying that it was a plan.

"Grant Simms will be here within the hour. Two at
most."

Maggie's lip curled. Grant Simms again. He'd been

at the local detachment for probably five years and he had a way of looking at Maggie like he *knew* things. When she'd pleaded Jen's case, she hadn't liked the way he'd watched her. Assessing. Like he was trying to figure her out, when her only motive had been to minimize the damage to her daughter. Jen had made a mistake. Maggie didn't think it should follow her around indefinitely. She realized now that Grant had probably told Nate everything about last summer and he'd never mentioned it. More secrets.

"You trust Grant."

"Of course I do."

She pulled back a little. It felt too much like choosing sides and she needed to distance herself again. Being close to him made it too easy to forget the many ways he had wronged her.

She would rather they met somewhere else. But it was hardly fair to ask that of him when he was already popping pills for his headache. She'd do it, knowing that it would make things move faster and the sooner she could get her life back in order. The sooner she could put this all behind her, once and for all.

"I'll put some coffee on, then."

She left the room but turned to pull the door closed behind her. Before it was latched, she saw Nate already facing the computer again, his hand on the mouse.

He was a cop, a fugitive hunter, focused on the job. There was no room in his life for her. It was just as well she knew now before something happened she'd truly regret.

10

It was probably good Grant was coming. At this rate, the deep freeze would be full, and she'd have to send a care package to Jen. Maggie stared at the pile of dirty dishes on the counter and the cooling racks full of baked goods on the table. She was more upset than she'd initially realized.

Baking meant she could avoid Nate. She could distract herself from thinking about how he'd lied to her, how he was putting himself in danger again, how in danger *she* felt when he kissed her and touched her, lighting her body on fire.

Only the distracting wasn't working so well this time.

She was sliding the third batch of muffins out of the oven when the doorbell rang. She put the muffin tins on top of the oven and pulled off her oven mitt as she went to the door.

Grant Simms was on the other side, dressed in plain-clothes but with his issue sidearm in plain sight.

"Good evening, Maggie."

"Constable Simms."

She knew she sounded frosty and didn't care. She stepped back, holding the door open, the only invitation to come in that she offered. He stepped into the breach.

With Jen behind him.

"Jennifer!"

For a moment she wondered if Jen were in trouble again, but dismissed it. She had no doubt that Jen had learned her lesson. Still, what was she doing here?

"Constable Simms sent for me this afternoon. He wanted me to answer some questions about Peter Harding."

Peter Harding?

"Hey, Grant."

Nate's voice came from the stairs and the three of them turned to look up.

He was fully dressed, in jeans and a dark long-sleeved t-shirt that accented the breadth of his chest and the curved muscles in his arms. "U S MARSHAL" was emblazoned down the sleeve. He'd shaved, changed the gauze and tape on the bandage. For the first time since arriving, he had on a holster and his handgun was in it. All pretenses were officially gone. Maggie blinked. Everything was upside down. What was now reality seemed surreal to her.

When Nate got to the bottom of the stairs, he and Grant shook hands, the grip strong as their eyes met. And Maggie knew that despite her personal feelings, Nate and Grant were a team. They were cut from the same cloth, and she was oddly reassured.

"Hell of a thing, you getting trimmed."

Maggie's face blanched as the words seemed to bounce around. All the blood drained from her head, leaving her spinning as Jen's and Nate's faces blurred. Nate frowned at Grant. The bandage glared white on the corner of his head.

"You didn't tell her?" Grant's voice echoed in her head. She knew what trimmed meant. She knew it meant he hadn't fallen and hit his head on a rock. Trimmed meant he'd been grazed by a bullet.

She heard Nate's voice, it sounded far away. "No. I didn't want to worry her."

She shut the door, closing her eyes, willing away the shock and numbing fear. Nate put his hands on her shoulders. She wanted to lean back against his strength but resisted. He'd lied to her over and over again. When would she learn?

"You were shot." She shook off his hands, knowing being touched by him made her vulnerable. She wanted to escape but didn't know how. He was blocking the door and Grant and Jen were watching it all. There was nowhere safe in the house. Yet how could she deal with this?

"Give us a minute, Grant. Jen, if you wouldn't mind waiting in your room, we'll call you when we're ready." Nate took charge, gripping her arm and leading her down the hall to the fragrant kitchen. Once there he squeezed her arms and bent his knees so he was looking in her eyes. "I was grazed, that's all."

"You were shot." She shook her head wildly, stopping when his grip tightened. "A man fired a gun at you with intent…the fact that he was slightly off the mark is irrelevant. And you wouldn't even go to the hospital!"

"I know a flesh wound when I see one, Maggie. And there wasn't time for a trip to the emergency room."

She'd had his blood on her hands.

"No time," she echoed. What did that mean? She pulled away but stopped by the kitchen table, standing next to the first chair. The one he'd sat in while insisting that she bandage the wound.

"I don't know what to say. I didn't want you to panic. And we can talk about this, but not now. There isn't time for it."

She nodded. This couldn't be happening. It was all becoming a big blur that she didn't understand. Things were moving too fast. She'd barely begun to assimilate that he was actually on the job. Now everything else came crashing around her. Grant was here. Jen was here, of all things. Maybe Nate cared, maybe he didn't. But the one thing that was clear was that he'd used her. Used her to get to this particular moment in time.

"Maggie, is there coffee?" Nate's voice was efficient but calm, and it grounded her. She turned her head, focused on his face. The truth had changed him. He was taller, somehow. More commanding. There was a force about him that was magnetic. He was a man to be reckoned with; a man who would do what was right. She should hate him for it but couldn't help but admire it.

"Yes, and fresh muffins."

"That would be great. We'd like it very much if you'd join us."

"What do you need me for?"

"It'll all make sense, Maggie."

Grant had only ever been coolly polite to her, and now they were asking, no demanding, that she accommodate their meeting.

Lord, she had so many mixed feelings over the matter she felt like making more muffins. Why couldn't they go back to the way it was before? It had seemed complicated, but it was simple compared to this. Before, it had been new and foreign. Now Nate was putting his life on the line and nothing she could say would make any difference.

Nate put his hand on hers as she retrieved a plate. The firm warmth of it heated her cold fingers.

"Thank you, Maggie. I know this isn't easy for you."

"No, it's not." She avoided his face, focusing instead on arranging the muffins on the plate.

"And I don't mean to make it any harder…so I'm going to ask you something in private."

Her hands stilled over the butter dish. There was more? How much more could she possibly take today?

"What could you possibly want to ask of me now?"

Surprise held her still when he took both her hands in his own. She risked a look up; his eyes held apology and understanding.

"You shared things with me these last weeks. Things about your life. And we…we developed an attachment. Yet…" he paused, looked at his toes, then looked up again.

"Just ask what you want to ask, Nate. We're too far along for niceties now."

"I find it hard to believe you haven't been involved with anyone since Tom."

Maggie's brows drew together. She couldn't read his face; he'd switched back into cop mode. What did her sex life, or lack of it, have to do with anything?

"What does it matter?"

The pressure on her fingers tightened. "Damn, I wanted to wait to ask you this at a better time. Maggie, have you been involved with anyone? Say, last summer?"

Last summer? She looked up into his face, her eyes widening with confusion. "You're asking me if I've had a boyfriend since Tom. Specifically, about a year ago."

"That's what I'm asking."

"I don't see what business it is of yours, but no."

She pulled her hands away and resumed arranging the tray. What reason could he possibly have for delving into *her* past? It was dry as dust. There hadn't been anyone since Tom. Not even close, until...

Until Nate. It always came back to Nate.

"You weren't involved with Peter Harding?"

Peter Harding? This is what this was about? It was the second time she'd heard his name tonight and Maggie's stomach dropped. Why in the world would he think she was involved with Pete? How could anyone? She had very real reasons to hate the man, not have an affair with him. Her fingers tightened on the edges of the tray.

She looked up at Nate, surprised to find him serious. "I have no use for Peter Harding. None whatsoever. He's despicable."

The relief on his face was so profound that suddenly

it all fit together. Pete was Nate's assignment. Pete, the man responsible for Jen's arrest, had shot Nate today. The thought made her knees go weak but she stood her ground. "He's who you're here for, isn't he?"

Had he thought she was involved all this time? She took a step back.

"Did you seriously think that I had an affair with a man like that?" And suspecting it, had he seduced her anyway? Or had he tried to get close to her, so she'd betray Pete? The very idea turned her stomach.

"I believe you when you say you didn't," he conceded. "Once I got to know you, I knew it couldn't be true. But I had feelings that I recognized might be clouding my judgment." His voice grew stronger. "But Grant is going to ask you and I wanted to give you the heads up. I thought it might be easier for you if it came from me first."

Grant, of course. She wondered if that was why he always looked at her with that cold, assessing glare. At least Nate had judged her correctly. She stared down the hall at the entrance to the den, her distrust growing. He'd let Jen go, but he hadn't been pleasant about it. Now he'd dragged her into this mess once again, when it would be best if it were all forgotten. She simply wanted to go on as if Peter Harding had never existed!

"What has Pete done?" She collected herself and put the plate of muffins in the centre of the tray. "After all you've put me through, you can at least tell me that."

"Bring in the coffee, Maggie. We'll talk."

She put the carafe on the tray and Nate took it from her hands. This was all happening so quickly. Only this afternoon she'd been humming and folding Nate's laundry and now she had the RCMP sitting in her den, talking about bringing in fugitives over coffee and muffins.

Nate put the tray down on the coffee table and Maggie poured three mugs of the steaming brew. She sat on the couch, surprised when Nate sat down beside her instead of in the chair closest to Grant, almost as if he were choosing her side. She stared at his thigh, lean and muscled even through the denim. She put down her spoon in time to see Nate meet Grant's gaze and give a small shake of his head. Grant shifted in his seat.

"Maggie," Grant began, "First of all I want to apologize for putting you in the middle of this. It was my idea completely. I certainly didn't mean to cause any upset."

She wasn't sure whether to believe him or not. Yet something in his tone rang genuine, something she hadn't heard before.

"You're after Pete Harding." She took a sip of the coffee, trying hard to appear calmer than she felt.

"Yes, we are." Nate broke in. "Your place was the natural fit. You're geographically close by, I could stay here legitimately, and your known connection to him helped."

"My connection," she echoed, lost. "I already told Nate I wasn't involved with him."

"Through Jennifer," Grant said gently.

Maggie turned and looked at Nate. "You did know." Her heart sank. She'd been aware from the first what he did for a job and she'd wanted to spare him the details of Jen's arrest. But he'd known all along. Of course he had.

He nodded. "I did. But it didn't matter. Jen told me about it anyway before she left to go back to school. She felt very sorry about putting you through so much trouble."

Maggie's eyes stung. Pete Harding was a waste of space in her opinion. Bootlegging and selling pot, petty stuff to most but she knew how it could cause lasting damage. Jen had been quiet when the whole arrest happened, unwilling to share much information at all and it had scared Maggie to death. She'd wanted Pete pulled in but she'd been informed at the beginning that there wasn't enough to warrant his arrest, so she'd focused on what was best for Jen. For months she'd lived in the same community resenting his presence and his above-the-law attitude.

She was glad Jen seemed to be on the other side of her troubles now. And yet here was Pete again, front and centre in Maggie's life. She huffed out a breath.

Grant spoke into the breach. "I'm glad to hear there was nothing going on with you."

Maggie turned her attention to Grant. "Why on earth would you have suspected such a thing? How could you? All I did was try to protect my daughter!"

Grant rested his elbows on his knees. "You're about the same age, you've been a widow for a lot of years. And you were very persistent in dropping the matter last summer when Jennifer was arrested. It looked like you were protecting him. We couldn't take chances. When we found out who he really was…we had to act."

Maggie put down her cup. "My only concern was minimizing the damage to Jennifer, and I was as much as told that there wasn't enough on Pete to charge him with anything. You haven't been here long, Grant, but if you'd talked to anyone in the community they would have told you point-blank that I'd never have anything to do with someone like Pete Harding."

"The only thing we had on file for you was Tom, and the questions brought up from his death…on paper it was very plausible."

Maggie looked at Nate. The eyebrow not hindered by gauze was wrinkled; like he was confused about something.

"Paper isn't enough." She turned her attention to her coffee cup.

"I know. Please accept my apologies, Maggie."

His words, his tone, his expression, were all earnest. Maggie looked at Nate again. He'd been thoughtful enough to ask her about it in private. Perhaps it made no sense in light of recent truths, but if Nate trusted Grant, it was good enough for her.

"Let's just move on, shall we?"

Nate angled himself on the sofa. "If you have anything you know about Pete that you'd like to share, that would be helpful."

Maggie couldn't think of a thing. "I only know he operates off his property. Booze and drugs. Wouldn't surprise me to find an illegal grow operation on the property somewhere."

Nate grinned suddenly, the expression lighting up his face. "Oh, we found it. Way more than the allowable number of plants. Thanks for the snowshoes, by the way. I don't think there's going to be much of a crop this year."

So he hadn't been going for walks, either. He'd been haunting the fields. "You were staking him out."

Nate nodded. "I took what I needed in my backpack and made do."

His backpack. Maggie now understood that he'd not only carried his lunch but very likely firearms and ammunition as well as surveillance gear. She fought against the sense of the surreal, tried to remain in the moment. It didn't seem possible that this was happening in her house.

Who was this man? The more she discovered, the more he seemed a mystery. How could he be the same man she'd kissed? The same man she'd told secrets to, the one who'd inspired feelings in her that no man had since she'd been married to Tom?

"You don't know anything more?"

She shook herself out of her thoughts in time to register the question.

"No, nothing."

"Then I think it's time to bring Jen in. If there's anything she can share that she didn't last fall, it could be helpful."

Grant went out and returned a moment later with Jen, who kept her eyes downcast and picked at a fingernail.

"Jen, honey, Constable Simms and…and Nate…" She still couldn't seem to bring herself to call him a marshal. "They just want to ask you a few questions about Pete Harding. You're not in any trouble. Right?" She aimed the last at Nate, giving him a warning eyebrow.

Nate nodded. "That's right. You haven't done anything wrong. Why don't you sit down, and we can see if you remember anything that might be important."

Jen sat on the sofa beside Grant and met her mother's gaze with red-rimmed eyes.

"I'm sorry, Mama," she said, swallowing.

Maggie's eyes misted. Jen hadn't called her Mama for several years and it took her back to those uncomplicated days of her childhood.

"You're forgiven."

Why it had taken nearly a year for them each to say those important words, Maggie didn't know, but as soon as they were spoken, everything changed. Her daughter was back. Really back. The relief hit her square in the chest.

"Jennifer," Grant began, "Last summer you didn't give us a lot of details and we think that you may have been afraid to say much of anything. I want you to forget that fear now. Nate is here, and I'm here, to take Peter Harding in for good. He can't hurt you, Jen. But you can help us so he doesn't hurt anyone else."

"What do you want to know?"

Jen's face was pale but somehow strong, and Maggie realized what a treasure she was. She met Jen's eyes and nodded.

"Did Pete ever threaten you?"

"He said that if I ever ratted him out I'd be sorry."

"Anything more specific? Did he use several girls to run his product?"

Jen shook her head. "Not that I know of. At first…at first he was kind of cool, you know? Then he got a little scary. I felt weird around him but by that time I was afraid to walk away. Then he…"

She stopped, turned away, and Maggie's heart stopped.

"Then he what, Jen." She tried to keep the shake out of her voice but failed.

"He showed me a trap door in the barn. It was where he hid his stuff. And he said if I did anything to cause trouble he'd hide me there, too."

Maggie's stomach tumbled clear to her toes as the ramifications covered her in waves.

Nate's mouth fell open and Grant's face turned red.

"Why in God's name didn't you tell me this last summer?" Grant's elbows came off his knees and his fingers flexed tightly as he raised his voice.

Jen sniffled. "I was too afraid! I figured if I kept quiet it would go away and it would be okay."

Maggie stood, crossed the room and pulled Jen into her arms. "Oh, baby," she whispered, holding her daughter close as she sobbed. "You should have told me. We could have stopped him months ago."

"You were so mad, I didn't want to upset you any more. And then you sent me away and I thought that…"

The childlike plea in Jen's voice touched her. In all this time, she hadn't considered that Jen might have felt turned away. She'd only considered her daughter's well-being. The backs of her eyelids burned.

"You thought what? That I didn't want you anymore?" Maggie put her hands on either side of Jen's face and looked her dead in the eyes. "Oh honey, I hated being without you. You're all I've got. But I wanted to keep you safe. To get you away from your troubles. I could never stop loving you! I certainly wouldn't ever punish you by sending you away!"

Jen's arms tightened around Maggie's neck and Maggie closed her eyes, feeling the tears trickle on her cheeks and not caring that Nate and Grant stood by watching. She'd sent Jen off to school somewhere else, tried to pretend none of it had happened, and all the while her baby girl had felt the sting of rejection. Had thought she wasn't wanted, which couldn't be farther from the truth.

Grant's voice interrupted quietly. "Jen, if there's anything else you have to tell us, now's the time. I wish you'd said something last summer."

Jen's voice came out in a hoarse whisper. "He said if I told anyone he'd lock me in there. I didn't think the cops would take it seriously, they'd think he'd only said it to scare me. But I saw the look in his eyes. I believed him."

Nate ground out an earthy curse, then the den fell eerily silent.

Whatever Pete had done, it had been enough that the U.S. Government had seen fit to send Nate up to get him. And they didn't do that for simple bootleggers. Maggie's body felt like stone; she couldn't move. Implications of what might have happened to Jen fell on her, heavy and cold. And for the first time, she was glad that it was Nate with her. Glad he was on the job. Grateful and…proud. Her arm tightened on Jen's shoulder as they faced the men together.

"I'm sorry," she whispered. "I have to know. What is it he's done? What's he charged with?"

After a moment's silence, Nate answered. His tone was clear, strong, and the words sent an icy chill up the backs of her legs.

"He's charged with three counts of kidnapping and sexual assault, and one count of murder."

A cry escaped her throat as she crumpled, sliding away from Jen. Nate's arm reached out, supporting her as shock rippled through her body.

Harding's threats didn't seem so harmless now. Delayed fear pulsed through her veins at what she could have lost. She'd lost everyone else. She couldn't have borne losing her baby girl, too. And she'd come closer than she'd thought possible.

Nate ignored Grant. Instead he put a finger under her chin and lifted it. When she looked up into his face, ashamed of what she'd done, frightened of what she'd just heard, what she saw in his eyes warmed her soul.

He would do whatever it took to make things right. He would protect her. He would protect Jen. She knew it in her heart. How could she hate him now for hiding the truth? Now that she knew all of it, she understood.

"It will be over soon, Maggie, I promise. Peter Harding will be gone from your life forever. You won't have to be afraid. Jen won't have to be afraid."

She closed her eyes briefly. "Thank you."

He pressed his lips to her forehead, and she let herself lean into it, just for a moment, gathering a little strength.

After a few minutes, she squared her shoulders. Nate had said that things were moving fast. That meant he and Grant had to be planning how to make the arrest. Her heart beat erratically, nerves bubbling over. Nate would be in danger. The best thing she could do now to help was make sure they had the time and space to plan, to prepare. To ensure there would be no mistakes.

"We'll leave you to talk now. You must have things to discuss."

"Maggie?" Grant's voice interrupted. "Jen isn't staying. I want her away from here, and safe. I have an officer ready to take her back to Edmonton as soon as we're finished here. I'm sorry."

"But..." Maggie looked up at Nate, then back to Grant. It would sound silly, insisting that she'd only just gotten Jen back. But now that she knew everything, she didn't want to let her go.

"Can't I stay here, with Mom?"

Nate's hand squeezed Maggie's and he looked down into her eyes. "It would be useless to ask *you* to leave, I know that. But we can keep Jen away from it. It would be one less thing for us to worry about."

Maggie knew that right now it was more important to keep Nate focused on his job. She looked up at Jen, raised an eyebrow. Jen looked stronger now, less frightened. Nate had a way of doing that and she loved him for it.

Jen wrapped her arms around herself. "It's okay, Mom. Once it's over I'll come home. I promise."

Maggie rose, her thigh tingling as Nate's free hand lingered over the fabric of her trousers. "I'll come and get you myself." She held out her hand and Jen took it. Maggie's knees trembled but she made herself take one step, then another, to the door. She avoided Grant's gaze as she left the room with Jen, closing the door behind her.

She leaned back against it. Yes, Peter Harding would be gone for good. But so would Nate.

And the thought of being without him made her very lonely indeed. She hated it almost as much as she hated the fact he'd be putting himself in danger.

A half hour later, after a quick cup of tea and a restorative, albeit brief conversation with her daughter, Maggie heard their voices in the hall; heard Nate say "that's it then." Maggie put down her teacup and held Jen's hand as she went to see Grant—and her daughter—away. She'd been remiss in her manners earlier, but she saw things differently now.

Very differently. Knowing what Pete had done, knowing how much trouble Jennifer could have been in… Grant deserved her gratitude and respect, certainly not the curtness she'd treated him to on his arrival.

When she walked towards the front door, Grant's eyes seemed to smile at her. She was no longer intimidated by his size, his bearing. Instead she was oddly reassured that he'd do everything in his power to make sure things turned out the right way. The animosity she'd felt for him all these months evaporated.

"Thank you, Maggie, for the hospitality—and for the information."

"You're welcome," she said, meaning it. She caught Jen in a quick hug. "Love you. Call when you get in. And I'll see you soon."

Grant lifted a hand in farewell and jumped the two steps off of the porch, Jen following behind.

"Constable Simms?"

He stopped. Maggie sensed Nate behind her and knew what she was about to say was as much for him as it was for Grant. "Be careful."

He smiled at her, a genuine, wide smile. She hadn't known his face could change that much. He looked ten years younger. "I'm always careful." His smile faded as he looked up at Nate, standing just behind her. "Nate... I'll see you at the staging area at five. Get some sleep, will ya?"

Nate nodded. "I'll be there with bells on."

He reached over and squeezed Maggie's hand. "I've got things to do. I'll see you later."

He left her on the cold porch, shivering in the frosty spring air and watching Grant and Jen drive away. More than ever, she had no idea what it was she wanted. She only knew she wanted it over.

———

By midnight she was sufficiently worried. She'd heard nothing out of Nate since Grant's departure, not a whisper of him moving about upstairs. The vision of his cut loomed before her eyes. He'd held it together during Grant's visit, but she'd seen the grey pallor beneath his usual healthy colour. She'd kept hoping he'd stir, perhaps come down to the kitchen for a snack. She'd bathed and changed into a pair of sleep pants and a t-shirt, but nothing. Her conscience nagged at her, telling her to forget her hurt feelings and check on him. The few hours of frenetic activity had subsided. And she was left feeling raw and open. It brought back so many memories she'd tried to bury.

She hated to wake him. He had to be up early and needed his rest. Yet...she was pretty sure he'd suffered some sort of a concussion.

She crept upstairs, although she couldn't figure out why. She was going wake him anyway, so why was she worried about making noise? Perhaps it was simply that now they were forced to tiptoe around each other. Hold a fragile balance. She didn't feel prepared to tip the scales in favour of the anger or the hurt she felt. The betrayal at his lies and the fear of the danger he was putting himself in, all mixed together with gratitude that he was there in the first place. None of her emotions matched up and she was completely off-balance.

She opened his door. It was dark inside and he was in bed, sprawled beneath the covers. One ankle curved outside the quilt, the skin of his foot pale in the muted moonlight pouring through his window. His lips were slightly open in sleep, the white bandage on his head a stark reminder of all that had transpired that afternoon.

She didn't want to touch him. Not now. It would do nothing but stir up memories and futile longings.

"Nate." She whispered it, willing him to wake. But he never moved, his chest barely rising and falling.

"Nate." She put a little more force behind it, to no avail.

Heart pounding, she sat tentatively on the edge of the bed. One of his arms was spread wide, his forearm sprinkled with dark hair visible under the edge of the blanket. She touched it lightly, the warm skin tingling on her fingertips. She'd never met a man like him. He was strong and deliberate, even in sleep.

"Nathaniel," she whispered, her throat tight.

His lashes fluttered up as he opened his eyes. The turquoise colour glowed darkly in the shadows, focusing on her face.

"Maggie," he murmured, the soft sound an endearment.

Her body warmed. Lies or not, the undercurrent of desire hadn't abated. She'd had time to think since the events of the afternoon, and even knowing there was no future for them, she understood his reasoning for secrets. He'd done it to protect her, to protect everyone, and had put himself in danger in the process. She didn't like it, but she understood it. He'd only done what he'd needed to do.

What she didn't understand was why he'd let things progress between them. Why he hadn't kept his distance. If he was here on business, why hadn't he kept it as business?

But was that what she really wanted? Then she would have missed out on the last few weeks, and despite the pain, both from dredging up the past and from learning about his deception, she couldn't bring herself to be sorry any of it had happened. She wasn't sorry that he'd made her feel more alive than she had in years. She'd never be sorry he'd kissed her and held her.

"I'll go," she murmured. "I wanted to make sure you were awake. You shouldn't sleep for long periods at once."

"Stay."

He hadn't moved. His foot curled around the blankets at the end of the bed, his arm stayed beneath the covers. But his eyes, and that one word, held her there.

"Don't," she whispered. She swallowed. Hadn't there been enough pretense today? He didn't need to act like there was still something between them. The truth was out, and it was bigger than both of them.

"Not everything about my being here was a lie, Maggie."

"How can you say that?" she whispered furiously. "It was a cover from the moment you called and gave your reservation to Jen." She turned away from his gaze. "Your interest in me was a cover."

She didn't want him. But even knowing it, her heart begged him to dispute it.

The arm shifted. His fingers reached up until they touched the skin of her face and it was all she could do to not close her eyes at the tender touch. She couldn't seem to move off the side of the bed, anchored there by the gentle graze of his fingertips and the intensity burning in his eyes.

"I lied about the professional side, because I had to, and now you know why." The backs of his fingers caressed her jaw. "But everything…personal between us was the truth. It was not part of the plan. I wasn't anticipating *you*."

"Why should I believe you?" She jerked her head away from his hand. She couldn't think, couldn't remain objective when he touched her this way.

"Because if you don't it means you were wrong." He didn't let her get away. His fingers curled over her ear and beneath her hair as he raised up on the opposite elbow. "Wrong when you felt this *thing* building between us. Wrong when you touched me, and I touched you. Wrong when you trusted me."

His lips curled ever so slightly into a smile. "You weren't wrong, Maggie. Those feelings—they're real."

She wanted desperately to believe him as his soft words wooed her. To believe that everything that had transpired—their confidences, the little touches, the way her heart soared when he kissed her—had been true. But she couldn't escape the memory of the cold steel tucked beneath his shirt today. Or the way she'd had his blood on her hands. She hated guns. Hated them with a passion. Even knowing he was a cop hadn't meant that much to her. He'd been on holiday, and for the brief time he was at Mountain Haven she'd chosen to ignore the fact when it suited her. He hadn't been on duty. He'd been someone else.

"I'm sorry about the gun," he whispered, as if he could read her mind. "You have to know I'd never hurt you. You have to know I'd do anything—anything—to protect you. Even lie."

"I feel used," she admitted, amazed that she still felt

she could confide her feelings. How could she be so angry and yet feel so close to him? Yet they'd always seemed able to talk. She remembered how he'd held her in the den earlier when she realized the depth of the danger Pete Harding represented. He had told her the truth when he could.

Perhaps in an odd way, that was the one thing that had been truthful between them. The ability to talk when it was necessary. He had a way of bringing out her secrets. Most of them, anyway. She still held a few close to her heart. She didn't want to see pity on his face. And without telling him, he'd never understand why she had reacted as she had to discovering his gun, or knowing he could have been killed.

His eyes searched hers. "I know you do, and I'm so sorry. And I did want to tell you. I even mentioned it to Grant, but he thought it would be better if I didn't."

He tugged with his hand. She was sitting on one hip and lost her balance, falling slightly to lay over his chest.

"Nate, I…"

He stopped her words with his mouth. First lifting his neck and seeking her lips, and once finding them, pushing up and twisting so that she fell beneath him.

It was different from the other times. This time it went beyond the sexual and hit her straight in her heart, and she didn't fight it. Maybe it was the freedom of the truth that changed it, maybe it was knowing it was all coming to an end, but despite everything he still had the power to do this; to make her feel like a desirable, loved woman. It was more than knowing he was younger, or the fitness of his firm body. It was in the way he touched her, like he couldn't help himself. Like she was something treasured.

But he was leaving tomorrow, and she wanted to absorb the feeling and keep it locked inside for safekeeping. To be able to look back and remember it when he was gone, to cherish it like she did the items she kept in her special box. For once, she stopped analyzing the pros and cons and let herself *feel*.

In the dark, on a rumpled bed, they were horizontal with his weight pressing her into the mattress. Her hands lifted, only to find the warm, bare skin of his shoulder, curved and dipped with hard muscle. Her fingers drifted lower, over his shoulders and back, stopping at a rough wrinkle. One of the scars he'd mentioned? She couldn't tell in the dark.

"This isn't a lie." His lips hovered over her ear before trailing down her neck. His weight pushed her deeper into the mattress. "What you do to me isn't a lie."

His mouth claimed hers again and she met it eagerly. She'd let fear stand in her way for too long. Now his time at Mountain Haven was drawing shorter with each fleeting moment. She'd been waiting for someone. Someone she could feel safe with. It shocked her to realize she still felt Nate was that man. Even after everything that had been revealed today.

He shifted slightly, his hand slipping over her t-shirt. He cupped her in his palm and her body surged from the contact, long-lost desire settling in her core. She arched, pressing herself more firmly into his hand, glorying in the feeling she'd nearly forgotten in her long abstinence.

He lowered his head until she felt his moist breath through the cotton.

A moan ripped from her throat and she gripped his hair with her hands.

And he stilled, his muffled cry of pain vibrating just below her heart. In the heat of the moment, she'd forgotten about his head and the gash that had unraveled everything.

"I'm sorry," she whispered. She was sorry she had hurt him. She was sorry they'd stopped, because being with him made her feel alive.

But it was madness and nothing good could come of it, no matter how much she craved him. He would still be leaving. He would still put himself in harm's way every day. She'd already been through it once. She couldn't deal with it again.

Nate didn't move. He simply dropped his head, resting it for a moment on the softness of her diaphragm. She closed her eyes and imprinted the feeling of him there on her soul.

"It's all right." His voice grated in the darkness. "We should stop. I promised myself I wouldn't do this."

Maggie suddenly felt very exposed, though she remained completely clothed. She put her hands on the bed, pushing herself upward a few inches. The fantasy was over, reality firmly back in its place. The need to protect herself overrode the longing to be with him one last time before he left.

Nate rolled to the side, propped up on an elbow. "I

promised myself I wouldn't let this go too far. I can't make love to you, Maggie. No matter how much I want to."

His explanation fell flat. He didn't really want her, and she'd been foolish to indulge in rolling around on the bed with him. Things were far too complicated. He probably thought she'd come up here with this very purpose in mind. Her cheeks burned at the thought.

"I don't recall asking you to."

Her icy words cooled the room considerably.

"No, you didn't."

She pulled away, stood beside the bed glaring down at him, angry at herself for falling under his spell yet again. He'd been the one to tug her down and kiss her first. To what purpose? Surely he didn't feel like he had to pretend anymore.

"What were you trying to do, anyway? Distract me from the fact that you've been pretending all this time? Or just smooth things over to soothe my hurt feelings? I assure you, I'm over it."

His nostrils flared but he didn't move from his position. "That's not it at all. I wanted to show you that despite everything, *this* much was real." His lip curled with the bite of sarcasm. "At least it was for *me*."

How dare he. He'd been the one to lie and pretend and she'd done nothing but be honest with him. Brutally honest, she remembered, her cheeks burning. Now he was accusing her of using him? Declaring his intentions to be pure while challenging that hers were anything but? And then pushing her away in the end anyway.

"When will you be wrapping this thing up?"

Nate pushed up off his elbow, sitting up in the bed. His brows pulled together in the middle.

"Tomorrow, then if it goes as planned, transport the day after. Why?"

Maggie smiled coldly. "Then I only have one more day of doubting every word that comes out of your mouth."

She instantly regretted the words, but gathering every last shred of self-pride she had left, she swept from the room, shutting the door behind her.

11

The coffee was brewed, but Maggie stared out the kitchen window, seeing little in the pre-dawn hours. She'd slept fitfully, waking every few minutes, worrying, thinking too much. Finally at four she'd risen, dressed, and put on coffee. She'd sleep later. She'd have lots of time for sleep.

Nothing made sense. She'd been mad about the lies, but she wasn't anymore. She was proud of who he was, but it scared her to death. She cared about him, more each day, but she wanted him gone. Wanted this over.

Wanted to come out of it unhurt, and the longer it went on, the more she was sure that was impossible.

Her head tilted as she heard sounds echoing through the upstairs. Nate was up. He was packing his things to walk away, leaving forever. She should be glad things hadn't gone further than they had. In her head she knew that was true. But all her heart felt was an aching loss at an opportunity missed; a return to a life that was lack-luster and plain. Most of all she was sorry she'd lashed out at him last night. He had enough to worry about without her throwing around accusations. It didn't solve anything.

She couldn't stand the thought of sitting here, waiting for news throughout the day. Listening for his footsteps when he came back…or didn't. No, it would be better if they said their goodbyes now.

He'd be down soon. Maggie took out a frying pan and got eggs from the fridge. The last thing she could do for him was make him a decent breakfast. It had nothing to do with any service she was being paid for; nothing to do with him being a guest in her home. It was, simply, the last caring act she could give him.

The eggs were delicately done when his steps echoed on the stairs. Maggie turned off the burner and went to the cupboard to fetch a plate. When she spun back around, she froze.

He was magnificent.

There was no other word for it and it frightened her almost as much as it exhilarated her. There was no hiding who he was from her this morning. He stood in the breach between hallway and kitchen, dressed in his customary jeans. But everything else seemed different. A long-sleeved shirt hugged the muscles of his chest and arms, and for the first time she caught sight of his USMS badge. It hung from a silver chain around his neck, a plain star within a circle with the words "United States Marshal" engraved in the perimeter. In his hands he carried more gear—a vest with several pockets, and two holsters. They made him seem so very large, imposing. Only she couldn't help but notice the dark circles beneath his eyes and a stab of worry went through her. He needed to be alert this morning. Was it her fault he wasn't rested?

"I made you breakfast."

It was all she could think to say. Anything more would open a door she didn't want to walk through today. They both knew what he was going to do. They both knew that he was leaving. There was nothing more to say without bringing up recriminations and regrets.

He put his gear on an empty chair and sat down as she placed the plate by his place. "Are you joining me?"

Food was the last thing on her mind, and she didn't think she could stomach it anyway. "I'll just have some coffee," she murmured.

Gone was the easy banter they'd shared over mealtimes. Gone was the subtle flirting, the friendly smiles and eye contact. The sound of his knife and fork were amplified through the kitchen and each clink was torture. She got up from the table and refilled his coffee cup.

"Maggie, I'm sorry about everything I've put you through. I've been incredibly unfair."

The emptiness crawled in again. His job came first and that was how it should be, she realized. And she didn't want anything permanent from him, so why did it hurt so much?

"Don't say anything. We both know it's what you do. We knew all along that this moment would come."

"This isn't easy for me, Maggie," he said quietly. "I wasn't counting on finding you."

Her fingers tightened on the back of a chair. He

didn't understand how she felt the need to pull back. To save herself from more pain. Seeing him hurt was bad enough. Finding out he'd been shot was another story. A fresh bandage shone on his forehead, a bright reminder of the consequences of his job. It was too close, too fresh. Even after all these years. She couldn't handle the danger. She knew it as surely as she was breathing.

"Maggie please. Talk to me."

She lifted her head, her vision blurred with angry tears. "And say what, Nate? You could have been killed! And don't shrug it off, because I know what it's like, okay? You're not the only one keeping secrets!"

His lips dropped open as her voice raised.

"I don't know what you mean. What secrets?"

She snorted, looking away for a moment. "What am I thinking. It was probably all in the background check you did."

"What on earth are you talking about?" He came forward, placing his hand on the countertop. "You're not making any sense!"

She put her hands on her hips. "Tell me you don't know, then. Tell me you don't have a clue that my husband died because he was shot on the job!"

The words came out so quickly she had no chance to hold them back. She'd never hidden the fact that Tom had died, but she'd also never let on he'd been shot.

His body stiffened. "He what? I swear to God, Maggie, I didn't know."

"How could you not know? Stop lying to me!"

The outburst rang through the silence and Nate stood up. "Maggie, I'm telling you truthfully. I didn't know about your husband. I only knew you were a widow. I promise. Grant didn't tell me anything more." He came forward, reached out to touch her. "It explains so much. Why you held back. Why you were so upset about the gun and the shooting. What Grant said last night about the file. I never knew. How did it happen?"

Maggie remembered the look of confusion on Nate's face the previous evening when Grant had mentioned Tom's death. Perhaps he hadn't known after all.

But talking about it still hurt. It still brought back all the bitter memories of that night and she had to swallow the bile that had risen in her throat thinking about what she'd been put through.

"He was a security guard for one of the oil companies. An activist didn't look kindly on their policies. Tom paid the price for that. We paid the price too, living with the inquiry, living without him."

"I'm so sorry, Maggie. Such a senseless way to lose a husband and a father."

She warned him off with a raised hand, blinking furiously. "Don't. Please, don't be kind. I can't handle any more."

The last thing she needed now was sympathy. Her eyes darted up to the clock, ticking along steadily as if they had all the time in the world. But they didn't. He had to go, and soon.

"You'd better finish your breakfast."

Her cold tone put an end to further conversation. Nate sat. Maggie didn't know how he could eat; her own stomach was tied in knots over the whole thing. She supposed this was an ordinary day for him.

Perhaps it was routine for him. Get up, get dressed, eat, and go to work. For her, this would never be normal.

Finally, it was over. Nate rose from the table and took his plate to the sink.

"Thank you, Maggie."

The words were deep and hushed in the quiet. Maggie closed her eyes, wanting to get goodbye over with and yet desperate to cling to every second she had with him.

"You're welcome."

Her throat thickened so that it was difficult to swallow. It was silly, she told herself, that she'd come to care so much about someone in a few short weeks. Someone who had misrepresented himself and lied to her. But she was smart enough to realize it wasn't that easy. Without intending to, Nate had broken through so many barriers she'd erected since Tom's death. She'd started to feel again – to want, to need. For a few glorious moments, it had been bliss.

But in the end, it wasn't worth the thud and she knew it.

"Nate, I…"

She turned but he was gone.

She found him near the front door. He'd shrugged into his vest and she could do nothing but stare. Never in her life had she been so glad to see Kevlar and she prayed it would keep him safe. Each pocket contained some piece of equipment he would need. The marshals crest appeared again on a flap that lay over his heart. As she watched, he propped his foot on a stair step and fastened a holster over his thigh, his movements practiced and efficient.

From his pack he took a handgun, placed it in the holster and straightened. When he did, he spied her watching him and their eyes clashed, held.

"You look so different," she whispered. He was a stranger yet not. He was the man she was attracted to, but so much more.

"This is who I am, Maggie."

"You're more than that, Nate. Don't think I don't know it."

Her lower lip quivered, she bit down to stop it.

Five more minutes. That was all she had to get through.

"I want you to take it all, Nate. When you leave this morning that has to be it."

His eyes fell on something by the front closet and she turned her head. His duffle waited, already packed.

It was what she wanted. It was. That didn't mean seeing him walk away wasn't going to hurt.

She met his gaze. He waited, strong and steady. How she wished she were brave enough to take a step forward, to tell him what it had meant to her, knowing him. To feel his arms around her one more time, to breathe in his scent.

"I've got to go, Maggie."

"I know."

They were whispering now. He shouldered his pack and picked up his duffle. Put his hand on the doorknob. And paused.

Maggie's body trembled. How could this be it? How

could he walk out with nothing more than a goodbye? Yet to say more would take more than she could give.

The bags slid to the floor and he reached out, pulling her close and pressing his mouth to hers.

Her heart leapt as she wrapped her arms around his neck, pressing as closely as she could though the thickness of his vest held them apart. The hard metal of the gun on his leg dug into her thigh; she didn't care. His tongue swept into her mouth and she met it, trying to tell him at last how much he meant to her despite the complications.

"Oh God, did you sleep at all," she wailed, pulling back and cradling his jaws in her hands, her thumbs touching the shadowed half-moons beneath his eyes.

"I couldn't. I could only think of you, Maggie." He crushed his mouth to hers again. When they finally came up for air, his voice was raw. "I wish you'd never left my room last night."

Her heart thundered. She'd started to wish it too, even knowing it was wrong. How was it that she could be so afraid for him this way—wrapped in Kevlar and strapped with weapons—and yet be so fatally attracted?

"I'm sorry, Nate. I'm not mad anymore, I promise." She gulped in air, trying to control the urge to cry. She couldn't go through this again. His lips touched her eyelids gently and his hands cupped her face. She knew this had to be goodbye. He needed to go, to get what he'd come for and finish it. There was no sense in going over again what couldn't be changed.

"I've got to go," he repeated. "I just couldn't leave without you knowing..." He lowered his forehead to hers. "Damn, Maggie. This wasn't just some assignment and we both know it. I'm sorry I hurt you. More sorry than you know."

"How can I be angry with you?" She tried to smile but it faltered. Soon his touch would be gone for good. "You did what you had to, Nate, I understand that."

"It wasn't just the job."

His breath warmed her cheek, and she closed her eyes, swallowing. Oh Lord, this was turning into the farewell she'd craved and dreaded all at once.

"I wanted to protect you, you and Jen. I see everyday what men like Pete can do. I'd die before I let him hurt either of you more than he already has."

Her blood chilled. The danger was real and imminent. Yet she was proud. "Do you know how rare you are?" At the shake of his head, she persisted. "You are. You take responsibility for what's right when most of us shy away."

"But…you want me to walk away."

"And it's the only thing to do." His thumb grazed her cheek and she fought back tears. "Now go. Grant will be waiting."

He picked the bags up again and opened the door. And just as quickly dropped them again.

And faced her, looking as serious as she'd ever seen him.

"I love you, Maggie."

The words stopped her cold.

He loved her? Maggie stepped away. No, no. They'd said all that they needed to say. He didn't mean it. He was supposed to be going to meet Grant. They were supposed to have their goodbye and she'd put her life back together. It was all supposed to be temporary.

But in a moment, he changed everything with those three little words. This was different. *Love* was different. Love hurt. She didn't have room for love.

She turned her back. "You're just reacting to today, that's all. What you need to do, what happens next. You can't love me; you've only known me a few weeks. You're just getting caught up in the moment."

"No, I don't think so."

Maggie faced him. This wasn't happening. He couldn't love her. It was supposed to be a beautiful goodbye, that was all.

"Nate, don't do this. I can't love you. You live thousands of miles away. And my life is here, with Jen."

"I know that." He took a step closer, unwilling to let her get away. "It's confusing, but it doesn't change how I feel. Or that I had to tell you."

Something inside her broke, a quiet snap that pierced the dam of denial. She'd told herself for so long that no one would ever love her again, but she'd been wrong. Nate loved her. It would never work, but simply knowing it filled her with a warmth she'd long forgotten.

She pushed it aside, that lovely joy and replaced it with the stark reality of what he did for a living.

"What is it you want, Nate?"

He came closer still until Maggie felt the cool wood of the banister pressing against her back.

"I want you. I want all of you, Maggie. I don't know how, but I can't let you go."

"You're talking about a future beyond today."

He was so compelling. His weight was balanced squarely over both feet, a pillar of strength and fortitude. He was everything a woman could ever want, so why was she determined to run in the opposite direction?

Because she knew what happened to people she loved, and Nate already faced enough risk every day. She wouldn't survive going through that again.

"Marry me, Maggie Taylor."

Her mouth dropped open for the briefest of seconds before she forced it shut again. Everything in her felt like weeping, only she couldn't. She couldn't fall apart now.

"Oh Nate, you know I can't." She turned away.

"Why not?" He grabbed her wrist and turned her back around.

Maggie set her lips, looking from his fingers circling her wrist up into his oh-so-earnest eyes. "First of all, my business and home are here."

"Sell it and start a new one. I can sell my house and we'll buy a new place on the water."

She shook her head. "Jen goes to school here."

"Bring her along. She can transfer her credits. Or she can go to school here and fly to Florida on holidays. Most kids would kill for spring break in the Sunshine State."

He was tearing down her arguments one by one and panic threaded through her veins. Why had he ever come here? She'd learned how to live her life her own way and he waltzed in changing everything. She couldn't handle that. Didn't know how to do it.

And the fact remained that she was a forty-plus

widow with a grown daughter and he was nearly a decade younger, just embarking on that phase of his life. It wouldn't be fair to either of them.

"What about children?"

Nate paused and Maggie knew she'd hit a spot. She grabbed at it, persisted. "Don't you want children, Nate? I already have Jen. I'm forty-two years old. And look at you. You're in your prime. Thirty-three and ready to start a family. And I don't want any more babies, not at my age. I'm sure of that."

"You're playing the age card. And that's not fair. I don't give a damn that you're older than I am. I never have, and you know it."

But she shook her head, stopping him. "No, I'm thinking ahead. It wouldn't be fair to you."

She skirted past him and into the den. It was true. She didn't want to have kids in her forties. Didn't want to be sixty and going through the teenage years, or trying to pay for college as she was retiring. But she couldn't blame Nate for wanting a family. It was another in a long list of reasons why it would be better to walk away. Perhaps one he could actually relate to.

"I don't want kids."

He followed her into the den. Maggie reached out and picked up a knick knack, turning it over and over in her hands. "You say that now, but…"

"No, Maggie. I don't want kids." His voice was firm, definite. "I've seen too many who weren't loved. I have nieces and nephews and I love them, but I've never wanted any of my own. I'd rather put my energies into helping ones who need someone to care. I'd hate to do that and not have energy for my own at home. That wouldn't be fair. So I'm okay with not having children."

He closed the gap between them. "Do you have any other roadblocks you'd like to erect? Because none of it changes the fact that I love you."

She could throw out the fact that he was asking her to uproot her life while his remained unchanged, but she knew she could never ask him to change who he was. Perhaps he'd change jobs, but he'd always be in law enforcement. There was no point even bringing it up. Not when she knew the real issue was that she never wanted to love and lose like she already had too many times in her life. Today had shown her that losing Nate would hurt. How much more would that be magnified after months, or even years of marriage? How could she stand waiting at home every day, wondering if he was alright, wondering if this would be the day he wouldn't come home? How could she stand to have her heart broken a second time?

There was only one way. And in her heart she silently apologized for it before she opened her mouth, knowing that while it hurt him, having to tell it was tearing her apart.

"I will never love anyone the way I loved Tom. I'm sorry, Nate."

He stopped cold and her heart wept as the light went out of his eyes.

"That's it then. I can't compete with a ghost."

"What did you expect me to say?" she whispered. "You know me better than anyone has known me in a long time. You had to know I wouldn't pick up and leave my life behind. Not for…"

The pause said more than the words ever could have.

She couldn't love and lose so horribly. Not again.

"Please Nate, don't make this harder than it already is." Everything in her longed to reach out and touch him but she couldn't afford the moment of weakness. "I can't love you the way you want me to."

"I can't argue with that." He ran a hand over his short hair, leaving little bits in spikes. "I can argue with logistics. I can't make you feel something you don't. I misread."

He shrugged his shoulders, inhaled. "That's it then. After we pick up Pete I'll be spending the night in town. In the morning I'll be leaving with Grant."

His eyes, dark with disappointment, caught hers one last time. "I know it's not nearly enough, but thank you, Maggie. For everything."

He turned and walked out the door, and she let him go, wishing he'd do it quickly now instead of prolonging the pain.

He stepped off the porch and towards the SUV that would take him away from her.

"Nate?" She couldn't help calling out to him as he lifted the tailgate and put his gear inside.

"Be safe."

He raised a hand in farewell and slid behind the wheel. Maggie closed the door and walked numbly back to the kitchen, putting his dirty dishes in the dishwasher for the last time.

She'd thought that once he was gone the tears would come, but they were locked deep inside, too deep for her to give them license. She sat at the empty kitchen table, closing her eyes.

After a time she rose and went to do the morning chores, anything to keep herself occupied. Returning to his room was another reminder of how close they'd come to making love last night and Maggie regretted how she'd acted. She wished now she had that beautiful memory to carry her through, but she hadn't been able to let down the wall she'd built around herself. When he'd stopped them, she'd convinced herself he was rejecting her.

But what she'd really been afraid of was herself. And now she'd hurt him without intending to.

But Nate had broken through her barriers anyway. She finished making his bed and turned, only to find the St. Christopher medallion he always wore. She sat on the edge of the bed where she'd lain with him, holding the heavy pewter in her fingers. Fighting the feeling of superstition that he should be without his good luck charm today of all days.

And when she realized how long she'd been sitting there, she fastened it around her neck. Tomorrow she'd put it in the trinket box she kept of reminders from those she'd loved. For that's what he'd done to her.

For the first time in fifteen years, she was in love.

And he was in love with her.

And now he was gone. Even knowing he wasn't coming back, she knew she wouldn't rest until it was over and she knew he was safe.

12

When the car door slammed, she leapt up in anticipation.

But it wasn't Nate's SUV. Instead, it was Grant's cruiser and he walked, alone, towards Maggie's front door.

"No," she breathed, a hand lifting to cover her mouth. Everything in her body went icily cold. She shook her head, backing away from the door. *Not again.*

Grant took off his cap and tucked it under his arm before ringing the doorbell.

She couldn't answer it. She pressed both her hands to her face, refusing to touch the doorknob. She couldn't listen to him say the words that she knew would come next. Oh God, she'd done that once before and it had blown her whole world apart. Tears seared the backs of her eyelids as she remembered the officer telling her Tom had been killed. And this morning...

The doorbell rang again. "Maggie?"

A single sob escaped. This morning Nate had told

her he loved her, and she'd told him that she wouldn't love anyone the way she'd loved Tom. She'd cast him off and sent him into a dangerous situation believing she didn't love him at all.

But she did. She loved him so much she refused to believe in a world where he didn't exist.

"Maggie, for God's sake, open the door!" Grant shouted now and for some reason the command jolted her to action and she turned the knob. And saw the smear of blood on his shirt.

He took one look at her face and his own gentled. "You're pale. Come sit down."

She shook her head. "Just say it, Grant. Please, just say it and get it over with."

His eyes were kind, so kind and she hated him for it.

"He's not dead, if that's what you're thinking."

Her breath came out in a rush. "I think I'll sit down now."

She made it to the first chair on the verandah and her knees gave out.

Grant knelt before her, chafing the sides of her thighs with his hands. The connection gave her something to focus on.

"Thanks to you, and to Jen, we found a stash of drugs, money, and weapons beneath the barn. And we were right in bringing him in, and none too soon. We found the cell. There were restraints. We're checking it now for DNA evidence."

The thought that it could have been Jen in there momentarily made Maggie's heart stop.

"But that's not all, Maggie. I'm just going to tell it to

you straight, okay?" He squeezed her hand and met her gaze squarely. "I came alone because Nate was shot and he's been taken to hospital."

"How bad is it?" She pulled away, twisting her pale fingers together, trying to hold it together and absorb everything Grant was telling her. Trying not to panic. Trying not to act like her whole world was crumbling around her.

"He's alive, but beyond that I really don't know."

Dread and fear froze her.

"I..." She halted; this was Grant whom she barely knew, yet she had to say it. "I turned him away this morning. I was wrong to do that, Grant." Her words came out childlike and contrite.

"I can take you to the hospital. Grab what you need and I'll wait."

Maggie nodded dumbly. Her only thought now was seeing Nate and telling him she loved him before it was too late. He couldn't leave her, not when the lie was there between them. Not before she had a chance to make it right. She got to her feet woodenly, stopping only to grab her purse and lock the door.

Grant opened the door to his cruiser and helped her inside. He got in the driver's side and called something in on his radio before reversing and pulling out of the lane.

He didn't spare speed and she was glad of it as they hit the main road. A call came back on the radio and Maggie tried to interpret it, but she couldn't seem to make sense of the words.

Grant answered back. Then turned to Maggie.

"Nate's stable for the moment, but they're airlifting him to Edmonton."

Maggie didn't move, it was simply another layer of shock. He was ill enough that he had to be transferred to a bigger hospital. He had to hold on until she got there, he simply had to. Flashes hit behind her eyes, of arriving at the hospital and finding Tom in a coma. All the things she wanted to say to him were meaningless. And then he'd been gone.

Nate had to hold on. He had to.

"I'm going to take you there, Maggie. Pete's in custody and not going anywhere. And odd as it seems... Nate's my partner in this. We'll go together."

Maggie sat back in the seat, surprised when Grant turned on his lights but not the siren, taking the highway north to the capital city. She didn't know what to say to him...her normal ability for small talk had evaporated.

But Grant suddenly seemed able to fill the gap.

"Maggie, I looked into what happened with Tom. It wasn't as simple as him just being shot. And a thing like that...I can see how it would change a person. I know you got to the hospital too late. And the investigation was no picnic...especially on top of all the grief you must have been feeling."

His clear eyes were unrelenting as he turned his head to look at her, like he could see her thoughts. The notion didn't unsettle her now, not like it used to.

"It's normal to be scared. And there are no guarantees. But...for what it's worth...I think it would be a crying shame to walk away from something, from *someone* who loves you as much as Nate does because you were afraid. You'd miss out on something wonderful, don't you think?"

Maggie tried to swallow around the lump in her throat. He made it sound so easy. Nothing about loving Nate Griffith was easy. When she'd said she couldn't love him like she had Tom, it hadn't been a complete truth. She did love him and it scared her to death. She loved him so much that she couldn't imagine losing him. That was what she'd meant and she'd deliberately let him draw his own conclusion as to her meaning.

"It can be damned lonely being a cop. Sometimes it's family that keeps us grounded. Wives put up with a lot, but…"

He kept his eyes on the road, smoothly passing a tractor-trailer and moving back into the right lane again. "Sometimes having that anchor keeps us going." He cleared his throat and looked back at her. "Think about it," Grant concluded.

There were so many questions. She had the bed and breakfast and a daughter and nearly crippling fears about being involved with such a man.

How badly had he been hurt?

And how could she let him do this alone?

———

At the hospital, Grant sidestepped a news crew which had already arrived. An officer being shot was news and Maggie had no desire to be captured on camera. As Grant snuck them through, Maggie stared at the tv crew open-mouthed, the lingering sense of déjà vu pervading again. A nurse directed them to the Intensive Care Unit and from there to a waiting room outside the closed, quiet doors.

When the time came, Grant went in first. Maggie tried to straighten her hair, make herself look presentable. But Grant was back within a few minutes, unsmiling.

"He's still unconscious."

"I want to see him."

Grant nodded. "The doctor says it's all right. I'll take you to him."

Once inside Nate's room, Maggie forgot all about Grant. Nate, her Nate, lay pale and prone on the bed. Tubes ran from his nose and more from his arm. His lashes were still on his grey cheeks, and as she watched, one finger twitched against the blanket.

But that was all.

"He lost a lot of blood," a nurse whispered, padding into the room softly and deftly adding a bag to his intravenous pole. "It's perfectly okay that he's not awake."

Maggie's shoulders slumped as she pulled up a chair to the bed, as quietly as she could. "Thank you. Is it all right if I wait?"

"We usually only let visitors in for a few minutes."

"I just want to sit with him. I don't want him to wake up alone."

The nurse looked at Maggie a long time, then at Grant, still in uniform, still with the stripe of dried blood.

"As long as you sit quietly."

Maggie nodded.

Grant stepped forward. "I'm going to get us some coffee."

She nodded dumbly; coffee was the last thing she wanted but didn't have it in her to argue.

And then the room was quiet, except for the soft beep of a monitor.

She looked at Nate's slumbering form. It was clear from the position and bandaging that the shot had hit his leg. A thousand questions flooded her brain…how bad was it, would he be permanently injured, did his head injury of yesterday affect his health now, did they get the bullet out, did it hit the artery…but all of them were subverted by a single thought: *Please don't leave me.*

Grant bought coffee; stayed a while, but in the end he had to return home. There was paperwork to be done and arrangements to be made now that Nate would not be transporting Harding himself. With a promise to come back as soon as he could, Grant left and it was only the two of them. Maggie chafed Nate's hand between hers.

"Hold on, Nate. Please hold on."

THE HAZE WAS WHITE, THEN GREY, AND THEN BLURRY shapes came into focus.

Nate swallowed—his mouth was bone dry—and realized that the beeping sound he heard wasn't his alarm clock, but a monitor that was attached to somewhere on his body.

He was in the hospital, and in that moment, he remembered exactly what had happened. The sound of the shot and the explosion of pain, and he instinctively stiffened. Only tensing brought the pain back and he forced himself to relax.

And when he did, he realized there was a mop of dark hair on the bed beside his hip.

Maggie.

He turned his head a half inch and tried to whisper her name, but nothing came out. He sighed and lay his head back against the pillow, closing his eyes, marveling that she was there, sleeping on his hospital bed.

He was a marshal, he knew that. He also knew that never in his life had he felt as strong a connection as he did to Maggie. He loved her, and it was different than anything he'd experienced before. Nothing about Maggie was easy. Perhaps that was why she was so perfect for him.

Why in the world couldn't she see that?

He sighed, knowing he couldn't place one iota of blame on her. Not after today. Before today he could have insisted that he wouldn't get hurt. He could have told her about all the cases he'd been on where he'd come out without a scratch.

But after today...there was no denying it. What he did had risks. And after the way her husband had died, hell, he couldn't blame her for not taking that on again.

He moved a hand until it could touch the soft silk of her hair and he rubbed a few strands between his fingers. She had said this morning that she couldn't love anyone as she'd loved her husband. But that wasn't what had made him walk away.

He had sensed her desperation and panic, and he

knew he couldn't pressure her into taking the chance. It wasn't fair to ask that of her, not after all she'd been through already. She'd already risked and lost everything. She'd fought him so hard this morning that he had known he couldn't hurt her more than she'd already been hurt.

Yet here she was. Waiting for him in a hospital room. He couldn't imagine how difficult this must be for her. He licked his lips.

"Maggie," he managed this time, his voice a rough croak.

She lifted her head slowly, one cheek red from being pressed against the blanket, her hair untidy. She began to tuck it behind her ears by what he knew now was force of habit.

"Nate."

As soon as she said his name, her eyes welled with tears and a few slid past her lashes and down her cheeks. To Nate, she'd never looked more beautiful. Her voice was soft and musical like he remembered. He'd heard it enough times in his head. Played it over and over like a favourite song, only he never tired of it.

He raised his hand, cupped her cheek, and closed his eyes.

Home.

This was how it felt, then. Everything he had known was missing came down to this very moment. Home wasn't his place in Florida or the Haven or a place at all. It was Maggie. Maggie was the home he'd been looking for.

He looked at her tear-stained face, drawn with worry and anxiety and he knew he'd been wrong to propose. Every argument she'd put up had been justified but easily disputed. Until the end. Maggie would never intentionally hurt anyone, so for her to say what she had, told him exactly how frightened she was. As much as he loved her, he knew that her feelings for him only caused her pain. The kindest thing he could do is accept her words and let her go.

"What are you doing here?"

Maggie linked her fingers with his. "Grant brought me. You're in Edmonton. You were shot."

His eyes widened. She'd said the last without flinching at all.

"I remember. Pete?"

"Is in custody. Grant was here…he brought me… but he left several hours ago to look after things. He's coming back in the morning."

Nate nodded. "I'm sorry I worried you. I'll be fine, though. You don't have to stay."

"Just try to get rid of me and see what happens."

Nate's mouth dropped open and for the first time, Maggie smiled.

It made him hope, even as pain shot from his leg into his gut. But hope was all he had, and he didn't want to squander a second of it. "I'll take you for as long as you'll let me."

"How does forever sound?"

Maggie laughed at the expression on his face. He hadn't been expecting that. But she'd had a good long time to think, and cry, and worry, and pray. And every single time she came up with the same answer: Any time with Nate was better than no time at all.

He winced and she stood up, glancing at the IV bags. "I'll call the nurse. You are nearly due for pain medication, I think."

He stopped her. "No, not yet. They'll put me to sleep. And right now I want to see you."

Her body warmed. All day she'd had images of what he was doing and they blended with the memories of the night Tom was killed. And then her fears had come true. And with them, truth—she loved him. But she hadn't known what to do with it.

Only hours spent at his bedside had shown her what was real, and right.

"Let me get you some water, at least," Maggie chided. "You need fluids. The doctor said so."

She wanted to kiss him but wasn't sure if it was the right thing or not. In the end she waited so long she just smiled and scooted from the room.

She was coming back from the ice machine when she spied Jen, curled up in a chair in the waiting room.

"Honey?"

Jen came awake instantly, standing up and tucking her hair in the same way her mother often did. "How's Nate? Is he all right?"

Maggie nodded, going into the room and sitting down next to Jen. "He just woke up. He's okay. In a lot of pain, but fine."

Jen's shoulders relaxed and Maggie's brows pinched together.

"I didn't expect to see you quite this soon. How long have you been here, waiting?"

"A few hours. Constable Simms called me at the dorm and told me what happened. Said maybe you'd like some company. But when I got here and peeked into Nate's room, you were asleep. So I came out here to wait." She reached over and took Maggie's hand in hers. "How are you holding up?"

"Me?"

Jen nodded. "Yeah. You. This couldn't have been easy for you, Mom. Not after Dad."

Maggie wiped her lashes; how many times was she going to cry today anyway? "When did you grow up so fast?"

"I dunno." Her old grin was back, impish. "Fast enough to see that you're in love with him."

Maggie's head snapped back to stare at her daughter. Jen's dark ponytail bobbed as she nodded her head. "You are. I knew when I came home there'd been something between you. You were different. And the way he held you last night…"

Maggie's heart thumped hard as she looked into Jen's eyes, ones so like her father's.

"How would you feel about that?" She posed the question carefully.

"Dang, Mom, you've been alone too long. And Nate's cool, you know? He's one of the good guys." Her cheeks pinked. "He took care of Pete, didn't he?"

"Yes, yes he did," Maggie murmured.

"Well, then, I think you'd be a fool to let him get away."

Maggie couldn't help but laugh a little. "You do, do you?"

"I do. Now, do you think it'd be okay if I said hi to Nate and then went home? I have a nine-thirty class in the morning."

"I think that would be fine."

They went into the room together, Maggie holding the plastic cup of ice chips and Jen with her hands in her pockets. But when she saw Nate, she went over to the bed, leaned over, and kissed his cheek. "Thank you," she said quietly. "Thank you for helping me. For helping us." She threw a quick glance at her mother.

"You're welcome," he whispered, his voice too hoarse for anything stronger. "And we owe you, too, Jen. I'm proud of you."

Jen squeezed his hand. "I'm going to leave you two alone, but I'll come back after class tomorrow. Do you want anything? The only thing worse than dorm food is hospital food. I can sneak it in."

Maggie swallowed thickly. It was so much like a family. Yet she'd turned Nate away just hours ago. Would he believe her now, when she was ready to tell the truth?

"Chocolate pudding," he murmured. "I love chocolate pudding."

Jen laughed. "Talk to you soon," she said in farewell, before closing the door behind her, leaving them alone in the dim light.

He patted the bed beside him. "Come here," he commanded, his voice still weak but warm.

She put the cup of chips on the table beside the bed

and perched on the mattress gently, trying to disturb as little as possible.

He took her hand in his. The hospital band chafed at her a bit, but his other hand was connected to the IV.

"Let's go back. Why don't you tell me what you meant about the forever bit. Because this morning you were prepared to never see me again."

It had hurt her to hurt him. And during the long day, waiting for news, she'd looked around her. What did she have at Mountain Haven? Nothing more than a list of excuses. A house, a home. A garden and a roof that needed repairs. She'd considered it her safe place but now knew she'd only been hiding.

She had a daughter who was already moving away, embarking on a new stage in her life. And what had Maggie done? She'd let her fears dictate her actions, letting her grief have control. She'd been so afraid of what might happen that she'd pushed away the one true thing.

Only Grant had shown up and had told her Nate was hurt, and none of it mattered anymore. Saying goodbye had done nothing to quell her feelings, or her worry. She knew in that moment that she wanted to stand by him *through* it, not pretend it didn't exist.

"You left, and I waited. It was awful, not knowing. But not near as awful as seeing your blood on Grant's uniform. Or hearing him say you'd been shot."

"I'm sorry I put you through that. I realized this morning that I had asked too much of you. It's never easy being married to a cop, for anyone. And after what you've already been through...I should have realized."

Maggie's heart skipped. "Are you saying you don't want to marry me?"

His eyes met hers, the blue-green glittering darkly in the pale light. "That's not the issue. The truth is, I should have been more sensitive. I knew all along how you felt and I pressured you anyway."

"Maybe I needed it." She straightened her shoulders. After all she'd been through today, it wasn't as hard being brave as she thought it would be. "I love you, Nate."

Saying the words, finally saying them, filled her with something so surprising she didn't know what to do with it. It was like everything in her expanded, awakened. There was power in it, beautiful power she hadn't expected.

She ignored the trembling in her hands and gripped his fingers. She longed to touch him, wished he weren't hooked up to monitors and medication. Instead she had to make do with their tenuous connection.

"It's true. I do love you, and I'm sorry I let my fear dictate how I acted. I think I need to explain," she murmured, her voice shaking a little. He'd opened his heart to her that morning, now it was her turn. And she wanted to do it. It didn't mean it was easy.

"Losing Tom was the hardest thing I ever did," she began. "Not only was he shot, but he killed a man in the process, and he was made out to be both hero and villain. Like my parents, I'd loved him and counted on him and he was suddenly gone. I had Jen and Mike to look after and I had to do it alone. I swore from that point that I would never give myself over to that sort of hope again. It hurt too much to lose. That's what I meant. I couldn't love like that again, not because I didn't love you but because the need to protect myself was too strong to give in to it."

"I knew that."

"You did?"

"All the other arguments were logical and easily remedied. But that one...I could see how afraid you were. And I knew you were too precious to hurt that way again. So I walked away, knowing at least I wouldn't be the one to cause you that sort of pain."

Tears flooded her eyes. "You knew."

"Of course I knew. Did you think I didn't get it? We got to know each other over the last weeks. I fell in love with you."

"When Grant said you were hurt, I knew without a doubt. I had to tell you that I had been afraid to love you. Afraid of what it meant to change my life for you. Afraid to live."

"Oh, Maggie."

"I want to live, Nate. I didn't realize I wasn't...didn't realize I could...until you came along. You changed everything. None of it matters without you."

"But I'm still a marshal. Look at me. I was really hurt today. I still have a job to do. And I'm not sure I'd be happy doing anything else."

"I'd never ask you to."

"What about being afraid? You were so angry when you discovered who I was. When you thought Jen might be hurt and when you found out I'd been shot."

"And I'll still worry. But I'll worry whether we're

together or not. Grant said something to me today. He said that sometimes family is the glue that holds you together. I want to be that for you. Don't you see Nate?" Her lip quivered but she kept on. "You always put yourself in danger. I want to be your safe place. The way that you've become mine. I always thought I was safer in my little corner. But I was so wrong."

"I love you, Maggie. And I'd do anything to be able to hold you right now."

Six inches lay between his body and the edge of the bed, but Maggie didn't care. She stretched out, aligning herself with his good side, her cheek resting against his shoulder. "Will this do?"

His voice rumbled, slow and sexy in her ear. "For now."

He was warm and strong and for the first time in nearly half her life she felt exactly where she belonged. Now, safe in his arms, the relief flooded her, and she finally let the tears come as she wept against his shoulder.

"Don't cry, Maggie. Please don't."

His voice, that smooth baritone with the hint of grit rumbled from his chest against her cheek. She shook her head against the cotton of his shirt. "I was sure of how I felt. But I also knew I might be too late. I was so afraid I'd be too late to tell you…"

"You're not."

He caught sight of the chain around her neck and the medal hanging from it. "You found my St. Christopher."

She nodded. "I was going to put it in my special box

of memories. Only it's not a memory. I'm not ready to give up on the future yet."

He squeezed her. "Oh, Maggie. I'm so glad." He released her and she lifted her chin so she could gaze into his eyes. Those beautiful, turquoise eyes that had somehow seen her from the very beginning.

"Is this a good time to ask you again?"

Her heart tripped over itself.

"Will you marry me, Maggie? We can figure the rest out later. Just say yes."

"Yes." And she shifted a little, pushing herself up on the bed so she could kiss him properly.

When she pulled away, she stayed propped up on an elbow. "Is your house big enough for one more? Maybe two?"

"You mean in Florida? You'd move there to be with me?"

A tiny smile worked its way up her cheek. "I would. I can sell Mountain Haven. And find a job there, or open a business. I think I might become very partial to palm trees."

"You would really give up your life here."

"I would."

"What about Jen?"

"Didn't you already solve these arguments this morning?" She teased him. "Jen's finding her own way. In another few years she'll be on her own completely. She's becoming an adult and making her own decisions. I'll leave it up to her what she wants to do."

He closed his eyes and Maggie was shocked to see a

tear gather at the corner of his eye. "Nate? What is it? Should I get the doctor?"

He shook his head. "No…it's just…" He opened his eyes again, struggling with emotion. "This morning when I was shot I thought I was going to die. And now here you are. It doesn't seem possible. I lied to you, Maggie, and led you on and did nothing but confuse your life. And here you are ready to give up everything for me. It doesn't seem right. It should be me making the sacrifices."

"No, Nate. You changed everything for me. Why should you give up your life? I'm not giving up anything, not really. Because I wasn't really living. I was only existing. You did that. Only you."

"You actually mean that."

"I do. I want to be with you. I know a part of me will always be afraid you're not coming back. But I can't sacrifice all the good stuff. Living without you isn't living at all. It's just putting myself in a box and hoping I'll never get hurt. And it's not what I want anymore."

"I want to touch you, do all the right things," he whispered in the semi-darkness. "I don't have a ring for your finger, but if you'll say yes I'll rectify that problem as soon as I get out of this bed."

"I don't need a ring to know what's true. All I need is you."

He traced a finger down her cheek with his free hand. "This sounds odd considering where I am. But there are things I can promise and things I can't. And you know that, Maggie. But I can promise you that when you're my wife I'll do my best to come home to you every night; to love you and protect you. Those things will never change."

"That's all the guarantee I need," she whispered, pressing her lips to his once more. "It's more than enough."

Read the first chapter of The Cowboy's Bride

"Miss? Wake up. Can you hear me?"

The deep voice came first, then Alex's vision gradually started to clear.

"Oh, thank God. Are you all right?"

Alex's eyes followed the sound of the voice as she looked up, dazed. Trying hard to focus, she found herself staring into the most beautiful set of brown eyes she'd ever seen. They were stunning, dark brown with golden flecks throughout, large and thickly lashed.

Men shouldn't have eyes that pretty, she thought irrationally, realizing with a jolt that she was captured in the arms of a stranger.

"Oh, goodness!"

The eyes crinkled at the corners at her exclamation, and she felt his hands on her arm and behind her back, helping her to rise.

"Slowly now. You fainted."

Really? I hadn't noticed. I was too busy being unconscious. She bit back the sarcastic retort when she saw the genuine concern in his eyes. He even made sure she was standing firmly on her feet before releasing her—and then stayed close, as if he didn't quite trust her to remain steady.

He would have fainted, too, in her condition and with this heat…and the lack of air conditioning in the convenience store hadn't helped much either.

"I'm so sorry," she blustered, brushing off her pants and avoiding his eyes. It had only taken a moment, but she could even now see him completely in her mind. Not just the eyes, but thick, luscious black hair, just long enough to sink your fingers into and slightly ragged at the edges. Crisply etched lips and a large frame in a grey suit.

Someone who looked like him was so far departed from her world it was laughable, and she avoided his eyes from simple embarrassment. She stared instead at his shoes…shiny, brown leather ones without a smudge of dirt or a blemish. A businessman's shoes.

"No need to be sorry. Are you sure you're all right?"

She bent to retrieve her bag and purse. The first time she'd bent to pick up her dropped crackers, everything had spun and then turned black. This time she gripped the bench for support, just in case. To her dismay she realized that she'd spilled her apple juice and it was running down a crack in the sidewalk. She folded the top over on the paper bag, picked up the juice bottle and looked around for a recycle receptacle.

"I'm fine," she said, finally looking him in the face. Her heart skipped a beat at the worry she saw there. It had been a long time since anyone had been concerned over her, and he was a complete stranger, yet his worry was clear in the wrinkle between his brows. Gratitude washed over her for his gallantry. "I haven't even thanked you for catching me."

"You turned white as a sheet."

She chanced a quick look around. Any passersby that had seen her little episode were gone, and now people went about their business, not paying any attention to them whatsoever. Another face in the crowd, that was all she was. Yet this man had seen her distress and had come to her assistance.

"I'm fine. Thanks for your help. I'm just going to sit a moment." She coolly dismissed him.

Solicitously he stepped back to let her by, and once she sat, surprised her by seating himself, as well. "Do you need a doctor?"

Alex laughed. Oh, she did, but a doctor couldn't cure what was wrong with her. "No."

The answer was definitive. By the way his shoulders straightened she knew he got the message loud and clear. Briefly she felt guilty for being blunt, so she offered a paltry, "But thanks again, Mr...."

"Madsen. Connor Madsen." He held out his hand, undeterred, inviting her to introduce herself.

She took his hand in hers. It was warm and solid and a little rough. Not a banker's hands, as she'd thought. Working hands. Solid hands.

"Alex."

"Just Alex?"

His eyes were boring into her and she stared straight ahead at the office building across the street.

"Yes. Just Alex."

It wouldn't do to encourage him. In the early June

heat, her t-shirt clung to her, the hem on the sleeves heavy on her arms and the fabric pulling uncomfortably across her breasts. And what had possessed her to wear jeans today, of all things? Apparently, it wasn't that uncommon for such a heat wave this early in summer, but for her, the temperature did nothing but compound the light-headedness and nausea.

Necessity had forced her wardrobe choice, plain and simple. Her shorts weren't comfortable anymore and at least in her jeans she could breathe. As silence fell, thick and awkward between them, the world threatened to tilt again. The feeling slowly passed as she took slow, deep breaths. "For the love of Mike," she mumbled.

He laughed, a full-throated masculine sound that sent queer waves through her stomach. "So, just Alex. Intriguing name. Short for something?"

She couldn't believe he was still here. After all, beyond the first fuzzy moment that she'd succumbed to his arms, she hadn't encouraged him at all. His attempt at polite conversation had done nothing but awaken an all too familiar sadness, the heavy weight of regret every time she thought of her parents. "My full name is Alexis MacKenzie Grayson."

"That's quite a name for a small thing like you." His eyes were warm on her and he twisted, angling himself towards her and bending a knee.

"Alex for Graham Bell and MacKenzie for the Prime Minister, you know? You planning on using it for the paramedics later? In case I faint again?"

He chuckled and shook his head. "You look much

better, thank goodness. But you spilled your juice. Can I get you something else cool to drink?" His eyes wandered to the convenience store behind them. "Perhaps a Slurpee."

Her stomach rolled at the thought of the sugary sweet, slushy drinks. Every teenager in a ten-block radius had been buying Slurpees today, and the very thought of them had Alex's tummy performing a slow, sickening lurch. She pressed her lips together.

"Or are you hungry? There's a hotdog cart down the street."

She stood, desperately trying to get some fresh air while exorcising the thought of greasy hotdogs from her mind. But she rose too quickly, her blood pressure dipped, and she saw grey and black shapes behind her eyes once again.

His arms were there to steady her, and she dropped her paper bag to the ground, the contents falling out as they hit the concrete.

His fingers were firm on her wrist as he helped her sit back down. "Put your head between your legs," he demanded quietly, and for some reason she obeyed.

Alex avoided his eyes as she sat back up moments later. "Sorry about that," she mumbled, completely mortified at the awkward silence that fell between them like a ton weight. This had to be an all-time low. Blacking out not once, but twice, in front of her own personal Knight in Shining Armor. And wasn't he annoying, this Mr. Perfect Chivalry, sitting there calm as you please.

She expected him to mumble his apologies and

hurry away. Instead he knelt and began picking up what she'd dumped on the ground in her haste.

Oh God. Her humiliation was complete as he paused, his hand on the plastic bottle of prenatal vitamins. His eyes darted up, caught hers. In them she saw sudden understanding. Now, of course, it all made sense. At least it made sense to *him*. She was still trying to assimilate everything.

"Congratulations."

Her smile was weak. He couldn't know. Couldn't know how her life had been turned completely upside down with a three-minute test only a few short weeks ago.

"Thank you."

He watched her carefully as he sat again on the bench. "You don't sound happy. Unplanned?"

She should end this conversation right here and now. He was, after all, a complete stranger.

"That's none of your business."

He had no cause to know her personal troubles. It was her problem. And she'd solve it. Somehow.

"I beg your pardon. I was only trying to help."

She grabbed the vitamins and shoved them into her purse. "I didn't ask for your help."

The pause was so long her scalp tingled under his scrutiny.

"No, you didn't. But I offer it anyway."

And who else was going to step up and give her a hand? She was alone, nearly destitute, and pregnant. She had no one waiting for her at home. *Home*, she thought sardonically. Now there was an idea. She hadn't had a real home in a long time…too long. Five years, to be exact. Five years was a long time to be at loose ends.

At present she was sleeping on the floor of a friend of a friend. Her back protested every morning, but it was the best she could do for now. She'd find a way, though, she thought with a small smile. She always did, and had since being left alone and without a penny to her name at eighteen.

Connor was a friendly face and the first person who actually seemed to care. Perhaps that was why she made the conscious choice to answer his question.

"Yes, this baby was unplanned. Very."

"And the father?"

She looked out over the bustling street. "Not in the picture."

He studied her for a few moments before replying, "So you're alone."

"Utterly and completely." Despair trickled through in her voice and she shored herself up. No sense dwelling on what couldn't be changed. Her voice was again strong and sure as she continued, "But I'll manage. I always do."

Connor leaned forward, resting his elbows on his knees. "Surely your family will help you."

"I have no family," she replied flatly, discouraging any further discussion of *that* topic. She had no one. Loneliness crept in, cold and heavy. Not one soul. Anyone she'd truly cared about in the world was gone. Sometimes she almost forgot, but now, faced with a pregnancy and no prospects, she'd never felt more isolated.

After a long silence, he spoke again. "Are you feeling better? Would you like some tea or something?" He smiled at her, friendly, and her heart gave a little foreign twist at this complete stranger's obvious caring and generosity.

"You needn't feel obligated. I'm fine now."

"Humour me. You're still a bit pale and it would make me feel better."

It was a lifeline to hold on to. It wasn't like her life was a revolving door of social invitations. "Tea might be nice, I guess." She looped her purse over her shoulder. "So where are we off to, Connor Madsen?"

"There's a little place around the next corner."

She chuckled a little. "You use that line often?"

"I don't believe I've ever used it before, as a matter of fact." He adjusted his long stride to her much shorter one.

"I wouldn't recommend using it again," she remarked dryly.

"You're coming with me, aren't you?" Connor shrugged out of his suit coat and draped it over an arm. "To be truthful, I don't spend much time in the city, picking up women. Or for any other reason, for that matter."

He was wearing a white dress shirt that fit snugly over wide shoulders then tapered, tucked into slim-waisted trousers. Alex hadn't believed men that good looking actually existed, and here she was going for tea with one. One who had already seen her faint. She shook her head with amazement.

"So if you're not from the city, where are you from?"

Small talk. Small talk was safe and not too revealing. She could handle niceties.

"I run a ranch about two hours northwest of here."

"Ah." Well, she certainly wouldn't have to worry about seeing him again after today. She'd be able to look back on it as a bizarre, fantastical dream. A knight in shining chaps, it would seem.

She giggled, then clamped her mouth shut at his raised eyebrow. "Is this the place?" she asked, changing the subject.

"It is." He held the door—more good manners, it seemed, seated her at a table, and went to get drinks.

The coffee shop was trendy and didn't seem to suit either of them. She pictured him more of a local diner type, drinking black coffee from a thick white mug while some middle-aged waitress named Sheila read the specials of the day. Despite his formal appearance today, she got the impression that he wasn't totally comfortable in a suit.

In moments he returned with two steaming mugs; one of peppermint tea and one with straight black coffee. The café didn't suit her much, either. She usually bought coffee from a vending machine or drank it thick and black from behind the bar, not that she'd been drinking much lately. Still, she was touched and surprised that he'd thought to get her something herbal in deference to her pregnancy.

"Thanks for the peppermint. It was thoughtful of you."

"I'll admit I asked the girl behind the counter for something un-caffeinated. And the peppermint might be, um, soothing." He handed her something wrapped in waxed paper. "I got you a cookie, just in case your blood sugar was low."

Alex wondered how he knew so much about the biology of pregnancy as she unwrapped the long, dry biscotti and tried a nibble. It seemed safe. A sip of the peppermint tea confirmed it. "Thanks. I think we're good."

His shoulders relaxed. "I'm glad. I'd hate to have a repeat of earlier."

She laughed a bit. "You'll have to find another method for your next damsel in distress."

Connor sipped his coffee, sucking in his lips as the hot liquid burned. "You seemed to need it. Plus my grandmother would flay me alive if I didn't help a lady in need."

"I thought chivalry was dead."

"Not quite." His smile was thin. "And this way I can procrastinate."

"I beg your pardon?" She put down her mug and stared at him.

"I have a meeting this afternoon. I'd rather spend the afternoon shovelling... Well, you get the idea. I'm simply not looking forward to it."

"Why?"

He avoided her prying eyes and stared out the window. "It's a long story." He turned back. "What about you? What are your plans for you and your baby?"

She took another long drink of tea to settle the anxiety brewing in her belly. "Our plans are pretty open.

I'm working, for now. Trying to figure out what to do next. It's temporary."

"You're not from here. I can tell by your accent."

"No. Ottawa."

He smiled. "I thought I sensed a little Ontario," he teased. "But there are so many easterners here now that for all I knew you could have lived here for years."

"Three weeks, two days and twenty-two hours," she replied. "I'm working at the Pig's Whistle Pub for now." She needed to find something else, something with better hours. But her tips were good and she'd have a hard time finding a boss as accommodating as Pete had been.

He didn't have to answer for her to know what he was thinking. It was a dead-end job and hardly one she could support herself and a baby on. She knew right away she'd said too much.

His brow furrowed a little and she somehow felt she'd failed a test. Which was ridiculous. He didn't even know her, and they wouldn't meet again, so his opinion shouldn't matter at all. She was working on coming up with a solution. Just because she hadn't come up with one yet didn't mean she wouldn't. Heck, she'd been finding her way out of scrapes for years. This one was going to take a little more ingenuity, that was all.

It was time to end this whole meet and greet thing. She pushed away her tea. "Listen, thanks for helping this afternoon and for the tea. But I should get going."

She stood to leave and he rose, reaching into his pocket.

"Here," he offered, holding out a card. "If you need anything, call me."

"Why would I do that?"

His face flattened and he stepped back at her sharp tone. "I'd like to be of help if I can. I'm at Windover Ranch, just north of Sundre."

She had no idea where Sundre was and had no plan of discovering the wonders of Windover Ranch, so she figured there'd be no harm in responding to his solicitude by being polite. She tucked the small white card into her jeans pocket.

"Thanks for the offer. It was nice meeting you, Connor."

She held out her hand, and he took it firmly.

Her eyes darted up to his and locked.

Another time, another place. She lost herself momentarily in their chocolaty depths. Perhaps in different circumstances she might have wanted to get to know him better. It was just her luck that she'd fainted in front of the first hot guy she'd seen in a good long time.

And it was the height of irony to meet someone like him, when she was obviously unavailable. She was pretty sure that being pregnant with another man's child was probably number one on a guy's "not in this lifetime" list.

"Goodbye," she whispered, pulling her hand away from his grasp.

Her steps were hurried as she exited the shop, but she couldn't escape the gentle and understanding look he'd given her as she'd said goodbye.

ABOUT THE AUTHOR

While bestselling author Donna Alward was busy studying Austen, Eliot and Shakespeare, she was also losing herself in the breathtaking stories created by romance novelists like LaVyrle Spencer and Judith McNaught. Several years after completing her degree she decided to write a romance of her own and it was true love! Five years and ten manuscripts later she sold her first book and launched a new career. While her heartwarming stories of love, hope, and homecoming have been translated into several languages, hit bestseller lists, and won awards, her very favourite thing is when she hears from happy readers.

Donna lives on Canada's east coast. When she's not writing she enjoys reading (of course!), knitting, gardening, cooking…and is a Masterpiece Theater addict. You can visit her on the web at www.DonnaAlward.com and join her mailing list at www.DonnaAlward.com/newsletter .

Find your next great Donna Alward read at
http://www.donnaalward.com/bookshelf